ARCHIE OF OUTLANDISH

Archie of Outlandish was created to be experienced through words, illustrations, and music.

Download your free copy of the Archie of Outlandish Original Book Soundtrack *at:*

NEWWRINKLEPUBLISHING.COM/SOUNDTRACKS

ILLUSTRATED BY ABIGAIL KRAFT
MUSIC BY JARED KRAFT

NEW WRINKLE
PUBLISHING

Published by New Wrinkle Publishing

Archie of Outlandish—Lynnette Kraft, Illustrations by Abigail Kraft

Archie of Outlandish Original Book Soundtrack—Jared Kraft

Copyright© 2016 by Lynnette Kraft, Abigail Kraft, and Jared Kraft

Interior Design and Cover Design by Abigail Kraft

1. Contemporary Fiction 2. Contemporary Fiction—Romance

ISBN: 978-0-9911109-2-6

www.NewWrinklePublishing.com

For Abigail, because she wanted a love story.

CONTENTS

ILLUSTRATIONS

Chapter 1

Outlandish wasn't your typical town. It didn't have cars rushing up and down the streets or loads of people hurrying to work. It wasn't a large, noisy city or a tiny, quiet one, either. It was an unusual, albeit charming town that sat on California's long coast, nestled in its own quaint spot between San Francisco and Monterey Bay. Because it was a coastal town, you might expect to see palm trees and colorful beach houses, and you would indeed find plenty of both, but what you might be surprised to see would be the large family of performing magicians spread out on the beach looking as though they'd fallen out of a Dickens novel (and drawing a good crowd, too). You might also wonder at the enormously sized fans that stood high above the rooftops. These fans were used to filter out the pollution that blew in from the larger, nearby cities. It was a very clever idea, dreamed up by a local, who was quickly becoming famous for his smart invention.

The only modes of transportation allowed in Outlandish (besides feet) were bicycles, roller skates, horse-drawn carriages, and small battery operated vehicles, which were owned by the town and used mostly by the city workers, as well as an occasional transport for the elderly. You could drive your car to the edge of Outlandish, but only as far as the parking garage that sat at the only entrance into town, and there your car would have to remain until you were ready to leave.

While it might seem an odd place, and indeed it was, Outlandish was an idyllic place to visit and an even better place to live. Not only was it safe, picturesque, and clean, but it was also filled with fine food, excellent music, offbeat entertainment, and one-of-a-kind shops.

If you were people watching you would see that most of the residents were over sixty. Retired men and women appreciated the safe streets and clean air, but they loved the entertainment and fine food. However, in the summer, curious people of all ages and walks of life came to visit this town that was known for its odd charm.

There were, of course, a few residents who weren't retired and those were (for the most part) the business owners, entertainers, and employees. One of those residents of Outlandish was Archibald Plumby, better known as Archie (much to his dismay). He was neither retired nor a vacationer. He was freshly twenty and still living at home with his parents. His father, Albert, was a businessman, his mother, Annella, a chef, and Archie was a writer. Their dwelling was a cheerful blue, two-story beach cottage that changed colors as often as his mother deemed it necessary, and that was about every two years.

Archie stood six feet tall and was a thin, one hundred sixty-five pounds. His face was hidden under a clump of bushy brown curls, and those curls hid in the shadow of the umbrella he always carried over his head. He wasn't sure if he was handsome, for only his mother had ever told him he was, and we all know mothers think their own children are the best and the most beautiful. But Archie was indeed handsome in his own way, although not many were able to get close enough to discover that for themselves.

Archie didn't carry his umbrella merely to keep dry (Outlandish wasn't a particularly rainy place). Nor did he carry his umbrella to shelter his skin from the sun, although he did have a fair complexion. Archie carried his umbrella because the sky was overwhelming to him—but not only the sky, for he couldn't even look up at an eight-foot ceiling without being afflicted with a panic attack.

Archie was born with this fearful condition. And his first few weeks of life were a bit of a nightmare for his mother and father—well, certainly for little Archie, too. Before he could voice his preference, he pulled blankets over his head and smashed his face against whatever was underneath him in order to avoid looking up. He screamed and thrashed and pitched a fuss, but his parents patiently endured those frightening beginnings, and after count-less visits to doctors of every sort, and receiving no answers, they settled into Archie's world and adjusted their lives to suit his eccentricities.

What most children do for fun, Archie did out of necessity. He played inside blanket forts, ate under-neath the dining room table, and slept in a short room, under a low canopy. Since nothing could be done to fix what was, by some, deemed a problem, Archie's parents embraced it and taught Archie to do the same.

Archie had always been a watcher as well as a writer and that was why he was employed at the local newspaper, *Stay Afloat*. His steady work, although only part-time, was in writing the observation column for the paper, but he also wrote (and updated as necessary), the *Outlandish Travelers Pamphlet*. He had lived in Outlandish his entire life, so who better to fill visitors in on all of the charms and appeal of his beloved town?

The regulars in Outlandish knew Archie, but mostly through his written words . . . and he never seemed to run out of them.

WELCOME TO
Outlandish!

Our motto here in Outlandish is "Lovely enough to do nothing and see everything. Lively enough to keep you entertained for days on end!"

Whether you're here for remarkable shows, exclusive shops and mouth-watering cuisine, or solely for pure air, quiet streets, and scenic views, we welcome you to our extraordinary town.

FIVE-STAR RESTAURANTS

1 The Jazz House
(Chef Jeremiah Salisbury)
Known for its exceptional salads and award-winning cardamom rolls—with a wine list and large dance floor to take you into the evening hours.

Flavors of the Earth 2
(Chef Annella Plumby)
Charismatic flavor blends and fresh tasting dishes are Chef Annella's forte. Set on the cliff, this restaurant offers a spectacular view of the coast.

SPECIALTY SHOPS

Hamlet's Salt Boutique 3
Brother and sister, Piccolo & Clarinet present a shop like none other—an ALL salt shop. It's spectacular to see all that can be done with salt. Go home with a local favorite: Chocolate Mint Sucking Salt.

4 The Poncho Bungalow
Ponchos of varying style in every color and pattern imaginable. Recently featured in *Mallory's Magnificent Finds*. Don't leave without your poncho!

ENTERTAINMENT

5

Tickle Me Pink Dinner Theatre
A stunning theater with a multitiered dining room overlooking the large stage. Fantastic shows and food all year long!

*The Pretentious Pindabrooks Magic Show
A mischievous bunch of shoddily dressed magicians—all from one huge family! The Pindabrooks are well-known, well-loved, and sure to entertain you.

6

Carriage Rides
Shire horses trot along in front of classic carriages and treat you to a unique view of Outlandish. But, perhaps the most unique element of the ride is the clown who will be your coachman.

*See performance schedule and locations on back cover

Chapter 2

It was Archie's twentieth birthday, and his mother had cooked him an afternoon meal instead of an evening one, because she needed to fill in at the restaurant for an ill cook that evening.

Mr. and Mrs. Plumby didn't often join Archie underneath the table for meals, but since it was his birthday, they moved all of the tall chairs away from the table and feasted together. Just for fun.

"The Coconut Shrimp was delicious, Mother. Really splendid."

His mother smiled. "But do you know why? See if you can distinguish the flavors, Archie."

His father put a finger up and said, "Ah! Let me do it."

Annella put her fingertips to her husband's lips and said, "No, no, no. I already told you, Albert. Now hush and let's see if Archie can figure it out."

Archie tilted his chin up, closed his eyes, and moved his lips around as if tasting the Coconut Shrimp all over again.

"Hm . . . shrimp, of course. Toasted coconut. Coconut milk. Aaaaand . . ." Tilting his head to one side, he continued, "Egg yolk. Cayenne pepper. Let's see . . . Oh! Scallions!" Eyes still closed . . . "Bread crumbs. Orange zest. Apricots . . . and . . ."

His mother watched him closely as if transmitting the secret ingredient to his mind.

Opening his eyes, he seemed to know the answer, but then when he opened his mouth to speak, the answer came out timidly and in the form of a question. "Almonds?"

"Yes! Very good, Archie! I tossed the coconut with almond oil before baking. You picked up a *very* subtle flavor. Impressive."

"Now why can't I do that?" Albert said with a pout.

"Because," answered Annella, "you don't savor your bites as you should. Flavors want your attention, Albert."

Albert laughed and shook his head, "Well, I *do* know the clam chowder had clams. Ha!"

"Now how about dessert?" Annella asked as she scooted away from the table and toward the kitchen.

"What have you come up with?" Archie asked.

His mother spoke with confidence, knowing it would please Archie, "Pistachio Cake with Pistachio Butter Cream Frosting."

Albert's eyes grew a little bit every time he heard the word *butter*, but when you added the word *frosting* to it, they grew even larger. Archie loved sweets, too, but not quite as much as his father did and his waistline proved it.

Archie's birthday meal was all very delicious . . . and filling; so much so, that Archie unbuttoned his pants to give his swollen belly room to breathe a bit.

"I think I'd better go for a walk," he said. "I don't know if I've ever felt so close to bursting."

His father said with an exaggerated, serious expression, "No, no. We can't have that. Can you imagine? Dying, on your twentieth birthday . . . from overeating of all things!"

Archie laughed, wrapping his belly in his arms as he did.

Albert continued, "And what would happen to your mother's career if word got out? Her days as a chef would be over for sure."

Archie continued laughing and said, "Father . . . please . . . stop."

"Go have your walk then," Albert said with a chuckle.

The beach was often a little cool, but since it was March, it was just a little bit cooler, so Archie pulled on his favorite orange sweater, slipped on his shoes, grabbed his large black umbrella, and headed out to the beach for an afternoon stroll. He walked close enough to the shore to feel the ocean water spray against his face and decided it was a little too chilly for that. As he turned to move away from the water, the wind, which was a little stronger than usual, caught his umbrella and threatened to make it topple, which would have been an absolute nightmare for Archie. He turned back toward the water and angled his umbrella so it would not be affected by the wind and decided to make his way back toward home in little sidestepping movements in order to keep his umbrella steady.

As he moved awkwardly along the beach, he saw a blond-haired lady walking toward him. *Surely she's not—*

For whatever reason, Archie had always been especially shy of the opposite sex. He could tell you many stories of close encounters . . . but he wouldn't.

"Oh gosh," he said out loud to himself, panicking.

Archie worried a little less about his umbrella and turned to walk a little more swiftly toward home (but he did still hold onto the left side of his umbrella canopy so the wind wouldn't catch it). He turned once to look back and saw the lady was moving a little faster, obviously attempting to catch up to him. He quickened his pace yet a little more in order to get away.

When he reached the door of his home, he turned to look and saw that she had given up trying to catch him but was still looking in the direction of his house. He moved inside, closing his umbrella a bit to fit in.

His mother was standing near the door when he entered, so she asked, "What are you doing, Archie?"

His head had been down, so he startled as he opened his smaller umbrella.

"Oh, um. Nothing, Mother. What are you doing?"

"The same as when you left a few minutes ago. Getting ready to go to work. I thought *you* were going for a walk. Why are you rushing back in so quickly?"

He knew he had been caught in the act of fleeing (it wasn't the first time), and so he did what he usually did; he tried to act casual, and as usual, he didn't do a very good job of it.

His mother walked over to where he stood and looked out the front window.

"Who are you running from now?"

"What do you mean?" he asked.

"Who is she?" she said pointing to the lady who was just turning to walk the other direction.

"I don't know whom you're referring to," he said without looking out the window.

"The blond girl over there? Were you talking to her before you came rushing in?"

Still avoiding the window, he quickly said, "Of course not. I was only cold. That's why I came back."

"Now, Archie. It's not *that* cold outside."

"The wind was brutal," he said much too dramatically.

"You ran from her, didn't you?"

Archie could feel his face flush. "Well. Why would I run from a female?"

His mother laughed. "A female? Really, Archie?"

"Well. She is, after all, a female. I mean, technically."

His mother's smirk bothered him, but he was so glad to see her shrug her shoulders and walk away that he decided not to say any more.

From the other room she hollered, "I'm sorry I have to work tonight. Especially since it's your birthday. It shouldn't be too busy though. Why don't you pop by for a bit? We'll visit in between things, and I'll bring out some extras from the kitchen."

"Well, I might come for tea, but please don't feed me another bite. I'm stuffed!" he said, showing that his pants were still unbuttoned.

Archie's mother walked back in to put a pair of shoes by the stairs and patted Archie's arm as she did.

"All right dear, no more food for you. Bring your notebook. Maybe you'll observe a thing or two for your column."

She chuckled as she walked back toward the kitchen, so Archie followed her.

"Mother. Why did you laugh?"

"I didn't laugh."

"Yes, it was just a little bit, but you did laugh. Why?"

"Archie. I didn't even realize I did. Why are *you* being so sensitive? What's come over you?"

Archie stood in silence for a moment and wondered, *What has come over me?*

Looking at his mother he asked seriously, "Now that I'm twenty, do you think I should look for more work?"

She looked at him thoughtfully.

He continued, "I mean, I don't know what else there is to be done in the way of an occupation. We both know my limitations."

Archie knew as soon as he said it, it was the wrong thing to say. His mother had always told him, "The only things you can't do are the things you aren't meant to do."

So naturally her response was, "Limitations?" and she said it as though she'd never heard the word before.

"That's not what I meant," Archie said. "You know I've never felt inadequate. I've accepted the things about me that are different. If I ever had the opportunity to feel sorry for myself, I don't remember it."

Archie's mother went to stand with him under his umbrella.

"Then what's changed? Aren't *you* satisfied with your column?"

"Yes," he answered quickly. "I am satisfied, but it doesn't pay very well, at least not much in the way of supporting myself, and I will have to support myself at some point."

Archie hesitated, "What if. Well . . . what if . . ." He dropped his head and sighed.

Annella lifted his chin. "What if what, Archie?"

Archie looked at his mother with one eye squinted, "What if I were to fall in love?"

Annella was surprised by Archie's confession. "Have you met someone?"

Archie quickly shook his head, "No, no. I haven't met anyone."

"No?" she asked with curiosity.

Archie shook his head and continued, "It's just that when I helped you cater the wedding last week, I couldn't take my eyes off of the bride and groom. I found myself wondering if it would ever be me."

"Why wouldn't it be?" she asked.

"I don't know. I want it to be. But what if it's not meant to be? What if I can't ever move beyond the Observation Column?" He rolled his eyes as he said it.

"Archie, the only thing that can stop you from having the life you desire is you. You have to pursue life as it presents itself to you."

Archie asked, "But should I be looking?"

"Perhaps," she answered, "but remember, your future will be established one day at a time just as each day you've already lived has been. There may not be any doors open for you today, but that doesn't mean there won't be any tomorrow. Try not to be anxious about it. You can't force things that aren't meant to be. See what I'm saying?"

"Yes. I see," was all he said.

Looking up at her son, she added, "Archie, falling in love is entirely possible."

A look of relief spread over his face, "Thank you, Mother."

His mother shook her head and asked, "Who was that girl, Archie?"

"Honestly, I have no idea."

Chapter 3

Archie's mother, known by most as Chef Annella, was one of three notable chefs who lived in Outlandish. Each of them owned their own restaurants and they'd all won awards for their dishes.

Annella didn't work at the restaurant because she had to, for her husband, Albert, was rich; Annella worked because cooking made her happy. She would have done it for free just to watch people react to the flavors of her dishes, but Albert, an entrepreneur, bought her the seaside restaurant so they could make a profit off of her talent. He would say, "It's just good business."

Albert wanted to call the restaurant "Annella's," but she insisted on calling it Flavors of the Earth, because flavors were Annella's life. She'd invested a good many years establishing what tasted good with what. Her admiration for food was slightly amusing, but she took it so seriously that no one would ever dream of laughing at her.

Flavors of the Earth only had one table inside with an umbrella, and it sat in the back corner by the kitchen. That table was Archie's, and it was where he sat reading his book on the evening of his birthday. His mother did come out of the kitchen on occasion, and his father even popped by for a bit while on an errand, but Archie mostly entertained himself.

He had just returned to his table with a cup of tea and stuck his head back in his book when he heard a voice say, "Hello. Is this seat taken?"

When Archie looked up and saw the same blonde from earlier in the day, he felt his heart quicken and worried he'd find himself in a full-fledged panic attack, so he purposely took some slow, deep breaths (hoping it wouldn't be obvious that he was trying to recover).

Though he knew his voice would certainly be shaky, he still attempted to speak. Unfortunately, when his lips parted, no sound came out. He opened his eyes a little too widely in surprise at his failure and then tucked his chin toward his neck.

Determined to prevail, he tried again.

"This. This table is private," he managed to say. "I mean to say . . . um . . . there are other tables available . . . ones you *may* sit at."

"Oh," she said, looking a little disappointed.

"Would you like me to locate one for you?" he asked. "This *is* my mother's restaurant, after all."

"Oh, is it?" she asked, sounding surprised.

"Yes," answered Archie.

She turned to take a quick look around the restaurant, looked back at Archie, and said, "So I can't sit here with you?"

Archie, caught off guard by her question said, "Well, *no*. I mean . . . there's no need for that."

Spreading his arms toward the room, he said, "Look. Tables. Everywhere."

Archie noticed red blotches beginning to appear on her face and neck.

"Are you all right?" he asked.

Her eyes narrowed a bit. "Ye-es. Why do you ask?"

He put his palms out toward his face and wiggled his fingers a bit. "Well, you're a bit . . . um . . . well, a bit, splotchy."

She put her hands up covering her lower face and neck.

Speaking through her hands, her words were a muffled, "Oh, I *always* do that."

"But you are all right?" Archie asked again.

"Yes," she said removing her hands from her face. "I do that when I'm embarrassed."

"Oh, did I embarrass you?" Archie asked.

"Yes, I guess you did," she replied with a little smile.

"I'm sorry," he said, dropping his head, feeling a little shame. "I'm afraid if I did it is because I am a bit shy of strangers. It wasn't my intention."

The lady put her hand out with a little reservation and said, "I'm Tallie. Tallie Greenleaf."

Archie hesitated in putting his hand out to shake as he still felt a little jittery, but because her hand was outstretched, he could think of no way around it.

"Ms. Greenleaf," he said, holding out his hand.

"Oh, no, just call me Tallie," she said, taking his hand.

Archie nodded.

Tallie stood waiting for Archie to introduce himself, but when he remained quiet, she asked, "And you are?"

Archie's body jerked as if coming out of a trance, and he said with a nervous laugh, "Oh, sorry. I'm Archibald Plumby."

Tallie smiled, "It's very nice to meet you, Archibald. Please forgive me for being persistent. I'm not stalking you. I do have a purpose."

"Oh?" said Archie.

"Yes, I'm a photographer-in-training, actually. I've been working with Gemma Perrelli."

Tallie waited for Archie to react to the name *Gemma Perrelli*, but his expression didn't change.

"You haven't heard of her?" she asked, shaking her head.

"No."

"Oh. Well, she's a very well-known photojournalist," she answered.

"Is she?" Archie asked.

"Yeah, anyway, I'm somewhere between her personal assistant and her student. Still learning the ropes, you know."

Archie nodded and asked, "And is she here with you in Outlandish?"

"She will be. Tomorrow. She's been in Europe. She sent me ahead to look for some new material."

"Why Outlandish?" Archie asked.

"You tell me. Why is everyone so enamored with this place?"

Archie surprised himself by saying, "Well, maybe you should have a seat then?"

"I was hoping you'd say that," she said with a look of satisfaction.

Archie stood and put his hand out to the chair across from him. Tallie sat down.

"You've not been here before?" he asked.

"No, I'm from Portland. Well, not actually from Portland. I'm staying with a friend there."

"I see."

"So Ms. Perrelli tells me Outlandish is known for being a little odd."

"Odd?" asked Archie.

"Oh no. Did I offend you?" Before he had time to answer, she added, "Ms. Perrelli just said Outlandish has its own sort of culture—that things are different here. That's all I meant."

Archie shrugged and said, "I've lived here my entire life. In fact, I've only been away from Outlandish a few times, and not for many years, so I don't really have a basis for comparison."

"Okay," Tallie said with a nod. "So why do you think people like Outlandish? I mean, people obviously love visiting."

Archie surprised Tallie by asking, "Do you find it odd?"

"Well, I've only been here a couple of days, but yeah, a little bit."

"Maybe I'm just a little odd myself and that's why I don't see it," Archie said while shrugging one shoulder.

Tallie smiled at Archie. "Well, I only just met you, so I wouldn't know, but who's *normal* anyway? I think we're all odd in our own way."

Archie said, "I quite agree," but then he looked up at the umbrella above him and turned his attention back to Tallie. "But then there's my umbrella. It *is* what caught your attention, yes?"

"Yes," she said with a smile, "I'll admit, it did. I've been here a couple of days and every time I've seen you, you've been underneath it."

"There are a lot of umbrellas on the beach. How did I manage to stand out?"

"Oh, it's just that you seem to be the first one on the beach in the morning, and what's visually appealing to me as a photographer is the look of the one man . . . under the umbrella with the wide shore . . . and the large sky."

Archie lifted his eyebrows, surprised by her attention to detail.

She put both of her palms against the tabletop, leaned forward, and said, "And if you could see it from my point of view, you'd totally understand."

"I think I can understand."

"May I ask where you get your umbrellas?" Tallie asked. "Every time I've seen you, you've had a different one."

"We actually order them from a man in London."

"London, really? Why all the way from London?"

"Mostly because of the way they fold up. They're much easier to manage."

"How does it fold up?" she asked.

Archie took his umbrella from the wall and demonstrated underneath the large table umbrella. Holding it up, he said, "See how it looks like it's inside out?"

"Yeah, upside down, too . . . like the handle's on the wrong side."

"That's right," he said. "What you're looking at is the interior of the umbrella, not the exterior. When you push on this," he said pushing up on the shaft's runner, "it opens down over you instead of out and up."

Pulling back down on the runner he added, "Then when you pull down on this to close it, the umbrella collapses from the outside in."

Tallie looked perplexed and shook her head.

"It's made my life much easier," Archie added.

"You make it sound like you need the umbrella on more occasions than most people."

Archie smiled and added, "The truth is, looking up into open space is quite a challenge for me. Impossible actually."

"What do you mean, *impossible?*" she asked.

"Well, I can turn my head and look up. It's not a physical inability. It's my mind. It doesn't quite know what to do with what it sees."

"So you need the umbrella as a shelter?" Tallie asked.

"Yes, that's it."

"Oh. Is there a name for it?" she asked.

"Doctors have told us it is similar to anablephobia—which is the fear of looking up—but most people with anablephobia are only bothered by large open spaces, like the sky or an auditorium. I can't even look at an eight-foot ceiling."

Tallie didn't want him to regret opening up to her. She had a feeling it wasn't something he did often. So in hopes of conveying a general curiosity without prying too much, she only said, "Interesting."

Archie nodded. "Most people with anablephobia can just avoid looking up. They walk with their heads down or keep their eyes lowered. I don't think there are many that require an umbrella."

"Could it just be a more severe case?" Tallie asked.

"Maybe. But typically cases develop over time or after a trauma. I seem to have been born with it."

"Will you ever be cured of it?" she asked.

"Not likely," Archie answered. "I've tried a good deal of therapies through the years, but here I am, still me. Right where I started. Well, not exactly where I started, I guess. I do cope a little . . . a lot better now."

"Do you mean you've learned how to live with it?"

Archie explained, "When I was twelve, my mother asked me if I would like to continue searching for treatment or just accept it and move on with my life. I decided I would like to accept it, and I've never given it another thought. It's just the way I am. I have no quarrel with it."

Tallie said in almost a whisper, "See, I knew there was something special about you."

Archie set the left side of his face down into his palm and raised his eyebrows exaggeratedly. "Oh no, not special. Just an additional helping of peculiar."

"Exactly!" said Tallie. "That's what I mean. That's why I'm here."

Archie moved his hand off of his face and clasped his hands in front of him. "So what *is* it you want with me?" he asked.

"I would like to photograph you."

"I'm afraid that will be impossible," Archie was serious. "Posing for photographs has never been my forte. You've seen how much I like attention."

"But would you be willing to let me get my photographs if I didn't bother you at all? I'd like to photograph you as you go about your normal routine. I promise you won't even know I'm there."

"What will you do with your photographs once you have them?" Archie asked.

"I'm not sure, but I promise not to use them unless I have your permission."

Archie sighed. "Well, go ahead and practice on me then, but I *can* promise you, if I see you taking them, I'm bound to run."

Tallie laughed, "Yes, I believe you will."

Annella walked out of the kitchen and over to the table with a fresh pot of tea, thinking she would share it with Archie. When she saw Archie sitting with someone (and wondered if it might be the same girl she had seen out the window), she decided she would serve them the tea instead.

She walked up to the table with the tea tray in hand and said to Tallie, "Hello. I'm Annella, Archie's mother."

"Oh, hi, I'm Tallie."

"It's lovely to meet you, Tallie. Are you new to Outlandish?"

Tallie heard Annella's question but was too delighted with her accent to answer. "You have an English accent! I love it!"

Archie looked at his mother and smiled. Annella smiled back at him before turning her attention back to Tallie. "Yes, I was born and raised in England."

Tallie appeared a little embarrassed and said, "I'm sorry. I've always had this thing for English accents."

Annella said, "Don't worry dear, newcomers often take notice of it."

"Oh good," Tallie said. "Anyway, yes, I'm new here, but I'm just visiting. Doing some work actually. I'm a student photographer."

Annella smiled, "Outlandish is a perfect place for a photographer. Isn't it beautiful here?"

"Really amazing."

"And how did you come to meet Archie?" Annella asked.

Archie didn't wait for Tallie to answer. "Oh, she came in looking for a table, so I invited her to sit with me."

Archie's mother looked at him in disbelief, but then said with a smile, "Well, wasn't that nice of you. Do you take tea, Tallie?" she asked, holding up the teapot.

"Not usually, but how can I refuse tea from an Englishwoman?"

Annella laughed while setting an orange teacup and turquoise saucer in front of Tallie. "I hope you'll enjoy it," she said pouring the tea.

"What pretty dish colors," said Tallie as she ran her finger along the turquoise saucer.

"Mother loves colors—*all* of them." Archie smiled at his mother.

Annella nodded. "Well, Archie, how nice to have someone join you for tea on your birthday."

"It's your birthday?" Tallie asked with surprise.

Archie was a little embarrassed by the attention and glanced at his mother with an accusing expression. Looking back at Tallie he said, "Yes. I guess it is."

"Let me guess," she said tapping her finger against her lip. "Twenty five?"

"No. Only twenty," Archie said through a grin.

"Oh wow, I'm older than you! I was sure you had to be older than I am." When Archie raised his eyebrows, she said, "I only meant you seem more *mature* than I am, that's all."

Archie nodded expressing doubt. "How old are you?" he asked.

"Well, not much older than you. Just twenty one."

Annella chuckled. "I'll just leave the tea tray and get back to work. You two enjoy yourselves." Annella touched Tallie's shoulder and said, "It was lovely meeting you, Tallie."

"Yeah, you too!" Tallie answered.

"Enjoy yourself, Archie."

Archie smiled and watched his mother walk away.

"Your mom called you *Archie*. Would you prefer if I did, too?" Tallie asked.

"No, I actually prefer *Archibald*, if you don't mind. I've never been able to figure out why parents name their children one thing and then call them another."

"Yeah, it is a little funny, isn't it?" said Tallie. "But I think it's like a pet name that's meant to make a person feel special. Don't you?"

"Yes," Archibald admitted. "I'm sure that's what it is, but still, I do like my full name and I don't get to hear it very often" he said with a chuckle.

"Well then, *Archibald* it is."

"Thank you," Archie said with a look of satisfaction.

"So now that I've met your mom," Tallie said, "I've solved a little mystery."

"Yeah?"

"Yeah. I noticed you say things a little formally and wondered why. Now I know."

Archie waited for her answer.

"It's because your mom's English, right?"

"I suppose it might be. Honestly, I've never given it any thought."

"Well, take it from me, someone who uses way too much slang, you speak very properly. Is your dad English, too?"

"No, Father is American."

"Oh," she said with some curiosity. "Well, your mother is stunning. I can see where you got your fair complexion."

"Yes, Mother comes from a long line of blond hair and blue eyes."

Tallie moved a little closer. "Your eyes aren't blue though, are they? It's a little dark in here. I can't quite tell."

"No, I have my father's hazel eyes . . . and his dark, unruly hair, too." He put both hands on his head as if to hide it. Tallie laughed and so Archie added, "I'm fairly certain I could grow a remarkable mustache like my father as well, but I think I'll hold off for a few years."

"Well, I don't think your hair is very wild, and I can totally see you in a mustache."

Archie turned his head away in embarrassment and mumbled, "Hm. Well."

Tallie sensed his uneasiness and decided to change the subject. "So what do you do, Archibald?"

Grateful for the shift in conversation, Archie perked up. "I write a column for the local paper."

"Oh? What column do you write?"

"The Observation Column."

"What's an observation column?" she asked.

"It's a column of stories written by . . . my observations."

"What do you mean?" Tallie questioned.

"I've always been one to watch activity. I see the things most people don't stop to notice. I'm not sure why. So when something catches my attention, I hold it there for a while and see what little story I can come up with." Archie glanced over at the restaurant entrance, looked back at Tallie, and asked her, "Would you like to see?"

"Sure . . ." she answered with a little hesitation, not knowing exactly what he would show her.

Archie grabbed his umbrella from against the wall, opened it up, and walked over to the foyer of the restaurant. He picked up a newspaper and walked back to the table. After sitting down, he opened the paper to his column.

"Here it is," he said, turning it toward Tallie.

"'Savory Sunscreen on the Beach.' What's that about?" Tallie asked.

"Well, I often make my observations on the beach." Archie said it seriously and then realized how luxurious his job sounded and felt foolish. "Anyway," he continued, "one particular day, I observed the bebumists on the beach were wandering, much more frequently, to the food carts. This continued for a few days, so I decided to follow them. I assumed there must be some new delightful food, but when I investigated, it was only the same vendors selling the same refreshments.

"The bebumists seemed especially drawn to the salty food carts . . . roasted nuts, popcorn, hot dogs . . . things of that nature. As I followed, I began noticing a very distinct smell of bacon. I went home and asked Mother to take a stroll with me just to confirm."

"Bacon?"

"Yes, but the smell wasn't coming from the food carts, it was coming from the bebumists."

"Wait. You've said that a few times and I don't know what that is."

"What *what* is?" Archie asked, confused.

Tallie said, "Be-bum—?"

"Oh! Sorry!" Archie said chuckling. "It's what we Plumbys call the people on the beach. You know...beach, bum, tourists?"

Tallie laughed hard at that.

"Beach bum tourists! That's hilarious! Okay, I'm following now. So the be–bumists smelled like bacon?"

Archie smiled. "Yes, so Mother asked a lady who seemed friendly enough, 'Do you smell bacon?' The lady said, 'Yes! I've been smelling it all day.' It took some more investigation, but we finally came to an amusing conclusion."

Tallie put her hand on Archie's arm and said excitedly, "The sunscreen!"

Archie nodded, "Yes, but you see, it was never meant to be. It turns out the sunscreen, which is made by a family here in Outlandish, was accidentally scented with one of their kitchen candle scents. The mistake wasn't discovered until Mother and I went to inquire about it."

"That's so funny!" Tallie laughed.

"I thought so."

Tallie slapped her hands on the table and leaned back in her chair. "I totally would have missed it!"

Archie answered. "I'm afraid I don't miss much in the way of a story. There are days I wish I could just look past things, but I see stories everywhere. I'm constantly giving titles to scenes."

"You should write books."

"They would need to be very short ones. My mind moves on so fast."

"Would you mind if I took a minute to read your article?"

Archie knew he would feel uncomfortable sitting quietly while she read his article so he responded nervously, "Yes . . . well. Why don't I just go and grab us some more tea?"

"Okay. Yeah. Thanks," she replied.

Archie watched Tallie from behind the swinging doors of the kitchen and only went back to the table when he could tell she had finished reading.

After Archie sat down, Tallie looked at him and said, "Archibald, your writing is so clever! Have you ever considered writing children's books? They're short." She laughed and added, "But seriously, your writing has a childlike quality to it."

Realizing he might take it as an insult, she added quickly, "I don't mean you write like a child. I mean you write in a way that would appeal to a child. I really did mean it as a compliment. Not everybody can write like that."

Nodding, Archie added, "Oh, don't worry. I took it as a compliment. The lighter side of life has always appealed to me the most, and actually, I *have* played at writing children's stories, a few of them. Of course, they're only at home on my bookshelf."

"They're my favorite," said Tallie. "I have my own little collection at home . . . although I didn't write any of them."

Archie looked admiringly at her. "Really?"

"Yes, really," she said smiling. "Do you illustrate your stories?"

"I do," he said. "Although I'm no artist. I've often wished I possessed both skills."

Tallie said, "Now, you *know* you've piqued my curiosity!"

Archie squinted as if trying to solve a mystery. He then cupped his chin with his thumb and index finger and looked at Tallie. "I don't think many of my stories are even worth reading. I wrote many of them when I was only a child myself, but you're welcome to read them . . . if you'd like. We could have a good laugh together if nothing else."

Tallie responded energetically by clapping and saying, "Yay! I'm excited to read them!" but afterward felt a little silly for her reaction.

Archie was actually entertained by her enthusiasm.

"So," she said in a decidedly calmer tone, "I'm having dinner tomorrow with Ms. Perrelli, but maybe we could meet back here after that?"

Archie tried to look as though he was considering his schedule. "Hm. Yes, I think I *am* free tomorrow night."

"Great! Does seven-thirty work for you?"

Archie looked at his watch (realizing immediately that it made no sense to do so), and momentarily forgetting her question said, "I think I'd better be getting back."

Tallie's confused expression reminded Archie that she was waiting for an answer, so he shook his head as if realizing his error and said, "But, yes, tomorrow night. Seven-thirty."

"Good. I guess I should be getting back, too."

Archie asked, "Where are you staying? I could walk you there."

"Oh, that's all right. If you need to get home . . . I'm in the circle at The Lupine Inn. It's just a little walk from here."

"I'll walk with you," Archie said.

Once outside the restaurant, Archie offered Tallie a place under his umbrella. "Shall we?"

Tallie noticed he had lifted his elbow for her, so she wrapped her arm around his and grabbed the shaft of the umbrella right above his hand.

"Does this work?" she asked.

"Perfectly," he said.

Along with a few of Outlandish's other businesses, Flavors of the Earth sat at the top of a short cliff. There were two paths up and down the cliff—one was a set of wooden stairs and the other was a winding road suited to those traveling on wheels.

Archie and Tallie took the stairs down to the path that followed the beach and eventually climbed a set of wooden stairs that led them away from the beach and into town. They walked in silence until Tallie stopped suddenly. Stepping out from under the umbrella, she looked up at the sky. Looking back at Archie she asked, "Archibald, can you come out from under your umbrella when the sky is dark?"

"If it's very dark, yes, sometimes I can. But it has to be a small moon. No street lamps."

"It must feel so amazing when you can!" Tallie said.

"Yes, it does. I have a place I go to just for that— away from the street lamps. But it's a little far, so I don't go often."

"I would go every night if I were you," she said.

"If you were me, you wouldn't need to go every night. I've grown quite accustomed to it."

Tallie regretted her words. "Of course. I'm sorry. I keep saying the wrong things. I just think it's great, you know . . . to have that."

Archie smiled easily at Tallie. "Please don't feel bad about it. I'm not at all offended. And yes. It is . . . *great*."

Tallie resumed her position under Archie's umbrella and they continued to walk in silence until they reached The Lupine Inn.

When they approached the door, Tallie ducked out from under the umbrella and said, "This is such a pretty little town. Have you ever stayed here in The Lupine? No, of course you haven't. You live here!"

Tallie laughed at herself and continued talking. "The floors are made of pebbles. Have you seen them? They're smooth, like river stones. But then there are rugs laid down over them. The rugs are so many different colors and textures. It's not like anything I've ever seen. I never would have thought to put them together, but they make the place so cozy. Everything in this town of yours is so vibrant . . . so . . . charming!"

Archie thought she was finished and began to respond, but then she surprised him by continuing.

"Then there's breakfast! They serve these pastries that taste like orange cheesecake. I'm in love with cheesecake. But I do feel guilty eating them for breakfast. They're definitely more like dessert."

Archie added, "The Lupine also has a reputation for having the best coffee in town."

"Oh? Well, I'm not surprised. It's so good, I honestly wondered if they added coffee flavoring or something. Is there such a thing as extra coffee-ee coffee? Ha!"

Archie was entertained by Tallie and decided he could listen to her all night, but instead of telling her so, he only said, "Well, it sounds like you and The Lupine are getting along splendidly."

"Yeah, I guess we are."

"You know. They buy those pastries from my mother."

"No way."

"Yes, and you're right, they're as delectable as you say. One of my favorites as well."

Tallie added, "You're so lucky to have a mom who can cook. How do you stay so thin?"

"Good question. My father tells me to enjoy it while I can. So I do," Archie said with a chuckle.

Tallie finally grew quiet, so Archie tried to fill in the void by saying, "I guess I'd better head back," but Tallie spoke at the same moment.

"Thank you for walking with me."

They laughed at their uncomfortable exchange but then had a second round of the same thing. Finally Archie scratched his cheek and said, "It's been a pleasure, Tallie."

Tallie smiled at Archie. "Yeah, it has."

Archie put his head down, shuffled his feet a little, and then turned and walked away. It was an awkward exit, but Archie wasn't sure how to avoid it. Tallie was caught off guard by his quick departure, so she wasn't sure what to do, but then she hollered, "Bye!"

Archie turned his head a little and smiled, and Tallie stood and watched him walk away under the light of the lampposts.

Chapter 4

The doorbell rang at the Plumby residence. Annella yelled from upstairs, "Will you get that, Albert? I'm just finishing my bath!"

Albert took off his reading glasses, put down his paper, and went to the door. When he opened it, he saw two women he'd never seen before. One of them smiled while the other looked at her watch.

"Good morning, ladies," he said with a smile. "What can I do for you?"

"Hi. Are you Archibald's dad?"

"Yes," answered Albert.

"My name is Tallie. This is Ms. Perrelli. Is Archibald at home?"

"Yes, Archie's here. Come in."

Albert walked the ladies to the dining area. Archie was underneath the table having his breakfast. His father leaned sideways to be level with the table and said, "Archie, you have company."

Archie put down his plate on the floor, grabbed the umbrella that sat waiting for him, and stepped out from underneath the table.

Although there were two people, Archie only saw Tallie. He breathed in discreetly and exhaled through his nose. Being prone to panic attacks meant Archie was an expert at breathing techniques.

He then put out his hand. "Hello, Tallie."

Tallie noticed his hand was a little shaky, so she grabbed ahold of it quickly. She smiled and said, "Hi, Archibald! I'm sorry to interrupt your breakfast."

Archie stuttered, "No, no . . . no, it's . . . fine."

Tallie released Archie's hand and said, "This is Gemma Perrelli, the one I told you about."

It was then Archie noticed there was another person with Tallie. In contrast to Tallie's petite and delicate presentation, Gemma was tall—as tall as Archie was, although she was wearing three-inch heels. Her silky black hair was pulled back into a tight bun at the base of her neck. Her eyes were almost as black as her hair and were painted with dramatic make-up. She wore a low-cut, red silk tunic and against her chest hung a large camera.

While Archie was still processing the scene, Gemma put her hand out and said in a businesslike tone, "It's nice to meet you, Archie."

Archie shook her hand, perhaps a little too energetically, and said, "Hello, Gemma."

"Ms. Perrelli, if you don't mind."

Archie was taken aback by her response and was also surprised at his desire to laugh. He looked at Tallie, and she looked away, embarrassed.

Turning back to Gemma Perrelli, Archie lifted his chin and said, "Ms. Perrelli."

She seemed satisfied. "Thank you, Archie."

Archie quickly responded with, "Archibald, if you don't mind."

Tallie put a hand over her mouth to hide a smile.

Before Ms. Perrelli had an opportunity to respond, Tallie said, "Archibald, I told Ms. Perrelli you have a column for the paper, and she asked me if I would introduce you two. She was hoping you might help her make some connections."

Ms. Perrelli looked at Archie and asked a little too bluntly, "Why were you eating underneath the table? And *why* are you using an umbrella inside the house?"

Archie smiled at Tallie. "I take it you only mentioned the less peculiar . . . ?"

Archie's voice trailed off as his eyes met with Tallie's. It was the first time he noticed her pale green eyes. He remained lost in them for a moment, until Tallie, growing uncomfortable by the silence, turned her head away, hoping he would direct his attention back to Ms. Perrelli.

When Gemma Perrelli saw that she, once again, had Archie's attention, she wasn't shy about going right back to her question. "Do you always eat your breakfast *underneath* the table?"

Archie stood a little taller. "Yes, I do, actually. Lunch and dinner as well."

Ms. Perrelli expressed confusion. "Why?" she asked with a mocking chuckle.

Archie put up a finger. "It's kind of a long story. Maybe we'll leave that one for another time." Putting his finger down, but leaving his hand in the air, he nodded once and left it at that.

Ms. Perrelli replied, "I would actually love to hear your story. I am a journalist, after all."

"Yes, a *famous* photojournalist, I hear," answered Archie.

"You've never seen my work?" she asked.

"No, but please don't take it personally," he

said putting his hands up as if conceding. "I live a quiet life."

"Hm," she said almost without realizing. After a moment of silence she continued. "I understand you write the observation column for *Stay Afloat*." Before he had a chance to answer, she interrupted with, "Isn't that an adorable name for a newspaper?" Tallie jumped in. "I know. Isn't it great?"

Ms. Perrelli didn't answer Tallie. Instead she asked Archie another question. "What is an observation column anyway? I've never read one."

Archie looked serious. "What, you've never seen my work?"

She was obviously not amused by Archie's mockery.

Archie was surprised (and maybe even a little impressed) by his outburst of unrehearsed sarcasm and wondered if Tallie's presence had induced his sudden courage.

It wasn't until his father cleared his throat that Archie felt foolish and forced a serious expression. "I . . . I'm sorry. What was your question?"

"Your observation column?" she asked impatiently.

"Oh yes. Well, I was already writing personally about things I was observing, mostly on the beach, and my mother and father were very fond of my little pieces so they suggested I submit one for publication. The editor was impressed and suggested creating a column. I've been writing the column for two years now."

"I would love to read some of your work. Would you mind?" she asked.

"If you'd like to, though I'm sure it's amateur compared to what you're used to."

"Maybe we could meet later today?" she questioned.

Archie nodded. "How about the front porch at two this afternoon?"

"All right. Where is The Front Porch?" she asked.

"Oh, no. I mean, *on* the front porch," he said pointing toward the door. At this point, Archie wasn't trying to be sarcastic, but Ms. Perrelli looked annoyed and sighed.

She put her hand out and shook Archie's hand firmly. "I'll see you at two o'clock then, on *your* front porch."

Shaking her head, she turned to leave. As she exited the front door, Tallie turned and smiled at Archie and whispered, "Are we still on for tonight?"

From under his umbrella, Archie smiled and nodded.

"Bye, Archibald," Tallie whispered again.

"Good-bye, Tallie."

He stood at the door and watched as Ms. Gemma Perrelli and the blond-haired, green-eyed Tallie walked away.

The table on the porch had a large, low-set, yellow-and-white-striped umbrella. At two o'clock Archie waited there for Gemma Perrelli with a pot of tea and strawberry scones (his mother's suggestion). When he saw her approaching, he stood (although hunched over) and put his hand out for shaking— but a bit too early.

Hoping she hadn't noticed, he put his hand back down and waited until she was on the porch before offering his hand again.

"Hello, Ms. Perrelli."

Shaking his hand, Gemma said, "It's nice to see you again, *Archibald*."

"Yes," said Archie as he offered the chair across from him with a slightly shaky hand before sitting back down.

"Well, I see you're right where I left you... under your umbrella. Quite low, too," she said, looking up and seeming irritated by the short distance between her head and the umbrella.

Archie put his hand on his clump of hair and fiddled with it. "Yes, well, this is where I live . . . under umbrellas."

She looked up at the umbrella and then looked back at Archie. "Tallie told me a little about your issue after we left your house."

Archie said lightheartedly, "Oh? So now you know I was born with some uncanny desire to see things a little closer to my eyeballs?"

She lifted one side of her mouth into a smile. "I'm sorry for being so blunt in asking about it when we met earlier. I'll admit, I was caught a little off guard by the table ... and the umbrella and ... well, I'm also a bit impulsive. Certainly not known for my reserve."

"I know it's an odd presentation," Archie replied.

"How old are you, Archibald?"

"Twenty. Just."

"I thought you were young. I *like* young people! There are so many unexplored places in a young person's life."

Archie examined Ms. Perrelli a little more closely. "Don't you consider yourself young?"

"No. No. I'm not young," she said shaking her head. "After reaching thirty I think I actually felt youth leave me. You wouldn't believe the effort it takes just to complete a day."

Archie was stunned by her confession. "Considering your success, I'm *very* surprised to hear you say that. Don't you like your work?"

"Oh, I don't hate it. It's just what happens when you're past your prime."

Archie perked up. "I completely disagree!"

"That's because you're twenty."

"No, it isn't," Archie replied. "It's because I've lived with parents who have never lost their passion. My mother would convince you your theory is wrong. Her love for life is astounding. And she's a chef because it adds joy to her life. She's older than you, and she certainly isn't past her prime."

"Yes," she admitted, "there are a few like your mother. I didn't mean to sum up all of humanity. It's rare, though. I work with young people because the energy they exude is what keeps me going. It reminds me of who I once was."

"That's why you work with Tallie?" Archie asked.

"Oh, yes! Tallie is just discovering life. She has endless enthusiasm."

"Yes, she does," he said in almost a daze.

Ms. Perrelli looked at him with suspicion, and Archie quickly turned the conversation back to her. "And you don't? Have enthusiasm?"

"Well, I try," she replied.

"Why only try?" he asked.

She folded her hands in front of her. "I watched everyone around me reach a place where they seemed to lose something, so I think I always expected it would hit me at some point."

"Why didn't you resist it?"

She looked at Archie with narrowed eyes but didn't respond. Archie decided to move a slightly different direction with the conversation. "Well, at least you've found success. Did you always know you wanted to be a photojournalist?"

She laughed. "Success. Yes, I have had success, but, no, actually I studied horticulture in college."

Archie looked surprised. "Well, that was a step in an entirely different direction."

"Yes, I guess it was. It's just the door that opened for me, and it was at a time in my life when I was trying to establish myself. You know, I was having a hard time getting people to take me seriously.

"While I was in my second year of college, I met a man who taught me to use a camera. I enjoyed it as a hobby but began to get attention when I won a national photography competition. My career just sort of took off from there. The money was good, so instead of finishing college, I made it my full-time career. I've been at it for about ten years now."

"But you aren't happy?" asked Archie.

"Oh, I don't know."

Archie didn't know what to say.

Ms. Perrelli broke the silence. "Now enough about me! Did you bring some of your writing?"

Archie nodded, picked up a book from the chair next to him, and placed it on the table. "Here are some of my recent articles."

She pulled the book toward her. "And to think I expected a stack of newspapers."

"You probably did. But I'm a bit particular about things. I like them sorted just so."

"You probably don't want me taking your book for the night though, do you?"

"Could you return it tomorrow?"

"Sure."

"That will be fine then," Archie answered.

She opened up the book and read for a few minutes while Archie stared off in the other direction.

"Who encouraged your writing? Was it a particular teacher?"

Archie looked back at her. "My mother. She's always been my teacher."

"You mean you never went to school? Was it because of your . . . problem?"

"No, not at all. There are no public schools in Outlandish."

"Really! Why is that?"

"It's because Outlandish has very few children, at least as residents. They come with their families in the summer, but then they go back home when school begins."

"I had no idea."

"Yes, well, a school has been discussed, but most of the residents are happy to teach their children at home. The few who can't, or don't wish to, take their children to a neighboring community for school. Nobody really complains."

"Do you feel like you missed out though?"

"On what?" Archie asked.

"Well, on . . . oh, you know, the things that happen while a child is in school?"

"I'm not aware I missed out on anything. My life has been just as it was supposed to be. I've always had an insatiable appetite for learning. It's been quite easy for me . . . and for my mother . . . I think. I've learned so many marvelous things!"

"But did you have any friends?" she asked.

Archie was surprised by her question. "Of course I've had friends. I've spent most of my time with the regulars in my mother's restaurant. I've always been able to relate to adults, even when I was young. But I did have young friends as well. One of them is Luke Pindabrook. Have you heard of the Pindabrooks?"

"No. Should I have heard of the Pindabrooks?"

"Well, as a photojournalist, you should probably meet the Pindabrooks. They're fantastic magicians. Really, I'm sure you would be impressed."

She seemed a little excited. "Will you introduce me?"

"I'd be happy to."

"Wonderful. I'll look forward to it."

"So tell me more about you, Archie. Oh, I'm sorry—*Archibald*."

Archie put his hands up in surrender. "Ms. Perrelli, I do prefer, Archibald, but honestly, almost everyone calls me Archie, so you might as well, too."

"Are you sure?" she asked. "I only called you that initially because I heard your father say it."

"Yes, Father and Mother both refuse to call me by the name they gave me. It really makes no sense at all."

Ms. Perrelli laughed. "Well then, Archie, since you're being so agreeable, I guess I should be as well."

Archie didn't know what she meant.

"Go ahead and call me Gemma."

Archie straightened his back and said precisely, "Not . . . *Ms. Perrelli*?"

She laughed and revealed a very white set of teeth between her painted red lips.

Her laughter helped Archie relax a bit. He added, "Because I just want to make sure you aren't acting on impulse."

She laughed again. "Oh, I did say that, didn't I? That was good, Archie." But then her laughter grew so loud Archie actually felt a little embarrassed for her.

When she finally quit laughing, Archie chuckled a little, just so she wouldn't be self-conscious about the dramatic change in atmosphere. He picked up his tea, took a drink, and said, "So what has Tallie put you up to? I don't suppose you want to take pictures of me as well?"

Gemma wiped away a laughter induced tear. "It's not often a photojournalist comes to a town called Outlandish and finds a man who lives under an umbrella."

Archie squinted one eye. "No, I don't imagine you come across that combination every day."

Gemma smoothed her hair with both hands. "When Tallie told me about you, and that you did some work for the local paper, I only hoped you would provide me with some connections to the community. That was why we came to see you in the first place.

"You see, I came to Outlandish looking for something interesting . . . no, exceptional really, but when I saw you under the table and then Tallie told me about your problem, well, you became the thing I became curious about. So, yes, I would love to photograph you . . . at work, at play, under your table, under your variety of umbrellas . . ."

Archie shook his head casually.

"And why not? Your story would be beautiful told through photographs." She spread her hands out as if displaying something. "Picture this headline, *Under Umbrellas—The Man from Outlandish.*"

Archie set his tea down, put his hands on the table in front of him, and looked at Gemma. "Let me ask you. If you lived under an umbrella because you had a panic attack every time you looked up at an open space, would you want the world to know?"

Gemma frowned. "Well, I'm surprised to hear you say that. You seemed so confident until you said that, regardless of your problem. Why do you suddenly seem as if you want to hide it?"

"I'm not trying to hide anything, but I'm fairly certain the temptation to hide will quickly arise once my story is out and everyone who sees it tries to come up with a solution to fix me. You *can* see that?"

Gemma did not surrender easily. "Do you ever feel like your umbrella will keep you from experiencing life the way you want to?"

"No, not usually."

She continued. "It does limit you some though, doesn't it?"

Archie shifted in his chair and looked down for a moment. When he knew what he wanted to say, he lifted his head and spoke. "Ms. Perrelli . . . Gemma. If you were born with a set of undesirable circumstances, say you were born deaf or blind or perhaps you were born with a heart defect or born missing a limb, would you prefer to see your life as limited or would you hope to thrive within those boundaries?"

"Well, I don't know," Gemma said. "I guess I would hope there could be a miracle cure for me and I would be able to live a normal life."

"But what if there was no miracle cure and you were destined to live with those things? How would you want to view your life under those circumstances? "

"I suppose I would just live with them and do the best I could."

"There's your answer, and that's where I am. I was born needing an umbrella, and I have never lived a limited life nor will I have a limited future.

My life might be different than yours, and I realize my scenario is uncommon, but it is only a limiting circumstance if I allow it to be."

"I don't believe you," she said. "I think you would still like your miracle."

"I'll admit, I find your perspective a bit alarming," Archie said. "Is it that unfathomable to think that I might be happy as I am?"

Gemma seemed to be ignoring Archie. "Well, what if we might be able to work out your miracle? Would you be willing to try a little experiment?"

"What kind of experiment?" Archie asked hesitantly.

Gemma looked squarely at Archie. "What if this inability to live away from your umbrella *might* be remedied?"

"And so it begins," said Archie, throwing his hands in the air.

"Noooo, Archie. It's not what you think. I'm very good at problem solving, and I like coming up with ideas. Wouldn't it be worth a try, at least?"

Archie shook his head. "You know nothing of my situation, but you think *you* can find a miracle cure? I spent years of my life in therapies and eventually made the decision to accept my circumstances. Not every life looks the same, Ms. Perrelli.

Different doesn't mean less significant or with less potential."

Gemma persisted. "But what if together, we could go beyond science and therapy and just come up with a practical solution for your problem? Aren't you even willing to try?"

"No, I'm not. Have you not heard a single word I've said? You keep referring to it as my problem, but I assure you, it's no longer a problem."

Disregarding Archie's words once more, Gemma added, "But what about your future? How do these umbrellas fit into your future, Archie?"

Archie immediately thought of his mother's answer to him when he had questioned her about the possibility of falling in love. So he repeated his mother's words. "My life, thus far, has been lived one day at a time. And so will my future be."

"But what if? Will you always ask yourself that if we don't try?"

Archie had had enough.

"Ms. Perrelli, I'm sorry you're not satisfied with your life, but I don't want to be your experiment, and I'm very surprised at your inability to see that I am truly content."

Archie began to gather his things. Gemma said, "You know, I was born with an unusually short frenulum and had trouble with my speech for years, but with persistence and—"

Before Gemma could finish, Archie breathed in deeply and said calmly, "Ms. Perrelli, I'm pleased to hear you have overcome some of your troubles, but the answer is still, and always will be, no. I understand some people might want to fix me because they think I suffer, but please believe me when I say I'm not trying to change. Everyone faces difficulties. I'm happy with who I am."

As if their conversation had not just derailed, Gemma said, "I see you're leaving, but if you wouldn't mind connecting me with the family of magicians you spoke of?"

Archie opened his umbrella, stood, picked up his book, and turned to leave. "Have a nice day, Ms. Perrelli."

As he walked away, Gemma stood and started to apologize but didn't. Instead, she said to herself, "He sure showed me," and then she smiled with satisfaction—not over her success, but over his and then said loud enough for him to hear, "Gosh, I love young people."

Chapter 5

Archie waited for Tallie at Flavors of the Earth. When she arrived he wasted no time in asking (for fear of losing courage), "Would you mind if we spent the evening at my house? I started to bring my writing here, but it was such an armful, I thought I might take you to it instead."

When they got outside, Archie offered his arm (and umbrella shaft) and said, "Shall we?"

Tallie and Archie walked under the umbrella until they reached the Plumby residence where both of his parents were enjoying a quiet evening drinking tea and watching television.

"Mother, Father, you've both met Tallie."

Annella was barefoot and wearing a sleeveless green linen dress. She walked over to greet

Tallie by not quite kissing both cheeks, as the British tend to do.

"It's lovely to see you again, Tallie."

"You too, Mrs. Plumby. Wow, you look amazing in green."

Annella seemed flattered by her words. "Oh, thank you, dear. My mother always told me to wear green. She said it looked nice with my eyes. So *of course* I've worn green a lot through the years," she said with a chuckle.

Tallie examined the room around her.

"Your house is gorgeous," Tallie said. "All the white makes everything look so fresh and clean."

"I use the walls and floors like my canvas," Annella said. "All the pieces of nature look so much nicer against it. Don't you think?"

"I do," she said. "It's so inviting."

"I've always loved bringing nature inside," said Annella. "It soothes me."

Tallie glimpsed around the room and saw dried flowers and herbs hanging from a white beam, as well as hemp rugs, bamboo window coverings, a variety of baskets, and rugged pieces of pottery. Colorful bouquets of flowers sat on tables that were painted white and shells and rocks were scattered here and there.

"It smells wonderful in here," she said.

Albert chuckled, "You've got that right. If it's not the food it's the flowers. Always something to take a good whiff of."

Archie stood and listened as his mother and Tallie discussed their love for nature . . . and food . . . and the beach. But then Albert said with a chuckle, "Nella, let them get on with their evening," to which Annella replied, "Yes, you're right, dear. Go on, you two."

Archie led Tallie up the stairs to his room. The first thing Tallie noticed was the doorknob sat very low on the door. She pointed to it.

"Yes, I know it's unusual," he said, "and it only gets more so from here. When I open the door, you'll have to duck down to go in."

"Duck down?"

"Yes, quite low, too. There's a dropped ceiling you're certain to crash into if you don't duck. You won't be able to stand when you're inside. We'll have to sit, and . . . well, crawl. Sorry."

"Oh don't be sorry. I'm beyond curious at this point."

He opened the door and then ducked in and dropped to his knees on the wooden floor. Tallie giggled as she followed him in the same manner.

Once inside the room, Archie moved over to the bookshelf. Tallie followed.

"Here they are," he said pointing to his books.

Tallie sat cross-legged and looked, not at the books, but at Archie's room.

"Archibald, this is fantastic!"

Archie smiled.

"Seriously, who thought of this?"

"My parents did."

Pointing at the poles that framed his movable ceiling, Archie said, "Father used bamboo so it would be lightweight."

"Why does it need to be lightweight?" Tallie asked.

"Because it was made to be adjustable, so as I grew, the ceiling could move up." Pointing to the holes in the corners, he said, "Those holes are for the pegs that make the ceiling work like an adjustable shelf."

Putting both hands in the air as if filling the space in between Archie added, "Mother stretched the loose burlap across them so I could still have the light from the windows. Otherwise it would have been very gloomy in here since the windows are above the ceiling. I love having the natural light."

"It's so innovative," said Tallie.

"Yes, Father's always been good with stuff like that, and Mother has been very creative in helping me figure out how to manage."

"Why don't you just use your umbrellas in here like you do everywhere else?"

"Because I like having a place where I can move around freely while being able to use both hands at the same time."

"Oh, I didn't think of that. That makes perfect sense. But that makes me wonder, how do you manage when you need two hands in the kitchen, or other places?

"That's where my ridiculous umbrella hat comes in. Please don't ask to see it."

"Ha! Okay, I won't. But it sounds pretty great."

Tallie continued to look around at the rest of Archie's room. "I feel like a child hidden inside an elaborate fort. Oh my gosh, look at your bed!" She crawled over to it and pointed at it. "Do you mind if I . . . ?"

"Not at all."

Tallie lay down on the bed and looked up at the canopy. "Seriously, Archibald. I've wanted a canopy over my bed for . . . my entire life! You're so lucky."

When she tried to sit up to move off of the bed, her head hit the canopy, so instead she rolled off and landed on her knees. She then proceeded to crawl toward the bookshelf.

Archie was amused. Tallie resumed her cross-legged position. "Those are nice red shoes."

Archie looked over to the three pairs of shoes that stood by his dresser. "I actually never wore them out of the house."

"Why?"

"I'm ashamed to admit, I lacked the courage."

"Oh, did your mom buy them for you?"

"No, I actually begged Mother for them when I was twelve, but I quickly realized red leather shoes weren't a common choice for young boys, and I guess I chickened out."

"At least they make a nice bedroom decoration," Tallie said.

"True. I do still admire them, and I was so disappointed when I outgrew them. But I left them there to remind myself to heed opportunities rather than miss them."

Tallie shook her head. "What a mature thing to do at such a young age."

"Would you like to see my stories now?" he asked.

"Yes. Show me."

Just as he lifted a book off of his shelf, Tallie touched an item and asked Archie, "What are these?"

Archie picked up a piece of pink sea glass and handed it to her. "Mermaid tears," he said seriously.

"Mermaid tears?"

Showing mock surprise at her disbelief, Archie said, "Mermaids have had many things to shed tears over. Just think of how many sailors and captains have perished at sea. You think that's easy for a lady to witness?"

Holding the sea glass underneath her eye, she said, "A sad mermaid. I don't like thinking about it."

Archie chuckled. "Well, let me put your mind at ease. It's actually just sea glass."

"Really?" asked Tallie.

"Yes, and pink is a rare color. They say most of it comes from the depression era."

She put it closer to her face and turned it over in her hand. "Interesting. Is all sea glass frosted like this?"

Archie pulled down a jar that was full of various colors, sizes and shapes of sea glass. He handed it to Tallie. "Yes. It's the salt in the sea. It erodes the glass, reshaping it as well as frosting it."

Tallie poured a few pieces out into her hand. "It's pretty."

Taking a piece of the brown glass from Tallie's hand he said, "Humans pollute the ocean with glass, and the ocean offers it back as art."

"I love that!" It's true with so many things in nature, isn't it? Is there a lot of sea glass on this beach?" she asked.

"There's actually a beach farther north called Glass Beach. It's full of it, but there is some here. Would you like to try to find some before you leave?"

"I would love to."

"All right," Archie said. "But the savvy collectors check tide charts and search when the tide

is at its lowest. If you go after they've been, you won't find much."

"Well, then let's use the tide chart and search with the pros!" she said with excitement.

Since Tallie seemed to enjoy the variety of pieces in his collection, Archie spent the next thirty minutes or so handing her this and that off of his shelf and telling her stories about when and how he'd discovered each subject (although not every item had an elaborate story).

Archie reached to the top of his shelf and pulled down a large abalone shell. Handing it to Tallie, he said, "This is the last of my treasures. My personal favorite as well."

When he put it in Tallie's hand, he heard her gasp softly. He watched her slide two fingers along the smooth iridescent interior. Archie noticed she had become very serious. "The colors are spectacular, aren't they?" he asked.

"Yes. I've always loved abalone. Did you find this on the beach?" she asked.

Archie nodded. "I haven't seen very many here. And this one is pretty big."

Tallie held the shell with care, outlining it with her fingertips. She then looked up at Archie with a forced smile. "My mom loved abalone." Tallie lifted out a silver-framed, abalone pendant, which was hidden inside her shirt on a silver chain. "This was hers."

"*Was* hers?"

"She died last year. She was only thirty-nine."

Archie put his hand on Tallie's arm. "Oh, I'm so sorry."

"Thanks. I really miss her."

"And your father?" asked Archie.

"I've never known my dad. He left my mom before I was born."

"Brothers? Sisters?" Archie asked.

Tallie shook her head. "That's what makes it so hard. There's nobody to talk to. Nobody loved her like I did. Do."

They both sat in silence until Tallie said, "I'm sorry. I didn't plan to bring it up."

"How did she die?"

"What does everyone seem to die of these days?"

"Was it cancer?" he asked.

Tallie nodded. "I am glad she isn't suffering anymore. It was hard to see her so sick."

"I never would have guessed you'd experienced such a horrible loss," Archie said. "You seem so happy."

Tallie remained silent.

"I don't mean to make light of your pain. I can't imagine how horrible that would be."

"I know God has a plan for my life," she said confidently. "That's what keeps me moving forward. My mom would have wanted me to do that. It's what she did when my dad left."

"It sounds like you had a wonderful mother."

"I did, Archibald. She tried to stay alive for me. She fought hard and did everything humanly possible. She wouldn't talk about dying until I begged her to. And that was only a few days before she died. I really needed her to tell me what to do, but she was bound and determined to be here for me."

Archie felt a pang in his heart. He found himself thinking about his own mother and the thought of losing her made him so sad that he considered trying to change the subject. But he knew he needed to be sympathetic to Tallie's situation, so he took in a deep breath and mustered up the courage to say, "Did your mother give you any advice before she died? Any last wishes?"

Tallie pinched her throat like she might be working out a lump and let out a little, "Ugh."

"That was the wrong question, wasn't it? I'm sorry. I really don't know what to say. I lack experience . . ."

"No, it's okay," Tallie said reassuredly. "I'm glad you don't have that kind of experience. I wouldn't wish it on anyone.

"What was most important to her was that I not be alone. I guess because there was no other family, she worried about me. She told me to find someone that would be a good friend to me. Someone that would keep me busy and help me to move forward with my life."

"Have you found anyone?" Archie asked.

"Not yet. That was one reason I was so excited when I connected with Ms. Perrelli, but so far our relationship is strictly business, so I don't know."

"Anyway," Tallie said shaking off her feelings. "My mom also wanted me to pursue photography. She thought I had an eye for it."

"Do you enjoy taking photographs?" Archie asked.

"Yeah, I love it," Tallie answered. "But there are so many photographers out there. I'm not sure how I'll stand out. Actually, I'm not even sure I want the pressure of an actual photography job. I think I'd rather do it as a hobby. But unfortunately I can't live off a hobby."

Archie smiled. "True. But wouldn't it be great if we could?"

"It would be," she answered.

"How did you meet Ms. Perrelli?" Archie asked.

"You know," said Tallie, "she actually pursued me."

"Oh?"

"Yeah, it turns out we both live in Portland. She has her regular coffee place called Junipers, which my mom's friend, Patrice, owns. I'm actually staying with Patrice. She's been so good to me since my mom died. Anyway, Patrice covers her walls with my photographs. I'm sure only to be nice."

"Oh, I doubt that. Did Ms. Perrelli notice your photographs while having coffee?"

Tallie smirked. "Yes, but I think she only wanted to help me improve."

"If she did, she still must have seen that special something your mother saw."

"Maybe you're right," answered Tallie. "Anyway, I'm grateful for her help and I do think God opened that door for me, but everyone is a photographer these days. I have no idea how I'll ever get noticed."

"If Ms. Perrelli is as well-known as I understand her to be, maybe you've already been noticed."

Tallie smiled. "I guess I didn't think of that. Speaking of Ms. Perrelli, what exactly did you two talk about?"

"Would it be all right if we avoided that topic tonight?"

Tallie looked pained.

"Oh, I'm not bothered by her," he said. "She and I just don't see eye to eye."

"She does seem to know her mind, doesn't she?"

Archie shook his head. "Actually, I don't think she does."

"Why do you say that?"

Archie was silent for a moment. "I shouldn't say. You *are* her protégé."

"Yes, but I can think for myself," she added, lifting her chin.

Archie nodded once. "Well, I think her success made her wander from what truly makes her happy and now she's looking for fulfillment from other people's successes. I don't think she'll ever find it there."

"You don't think she loves photography?"

"I think she had accidental success on her way to pursuing something else . . . something she wanted more."

"But don't you think fate can look like an accident?"

"As in serendipitous events? Yes. I do believe that can happen, but I don't think that is what happened to Ms. Perrelli. I believe it was, as I said before, accidental success that led her away from what she was meant to do. If it was fate, I would expect her to be happy."

"Why do you think she's unhappy?"

"Does she seem happy to you?" asked Archie.

"I don't know," answered Tallie. "I guess I've never really thought about it. She definitely seems confident."

Archie looked a bit apologetic and said, "You know what? I shouldn't have made assumptions about Ms. Perrelli. She did that with me and I didn't appreciate it, so I . . . guess she wouldn't, either."

"She told me she upset you," Tallie said.

"Did she?"

Tallie nodded. "I think she means well. I hope."

Archie doubted that. "I guess. Now why don't I show you my stories?"

"Yes," said Tallie. "Why don't you?"

Chapter 6

Sundays were for mingling in Outlandish. Most residents in the community met on the beach for a potluck brunch at 10:00 a.m., which lasted until around noon, at which time everyone went home for their afternoon naps. At 3:00 p.m., those who wished to (not nearly as many as attended the brunch) met in what was referred to as Central Circle, an actual circle in the center of Outlandish.

The center of town was as vivid and beautiful as the rest of Outlandish. Brightly painted buildings covered in decorated signs surrounded the circle. Flowers overflowed and hung from every lamppost, but the real showstopper was the mosaic fountain that sat in the center of it all. While it *was* something to stop and stare at, it was only because it was enormous and the shape of it was unidentifiable. The water shot up out of the top of it, and it might have been at least somewhat pretty if the mosaic tiles had been placed in a particular design or pattern, but instead, members of the community placed the tiles in random fashion, so it was mostly just bizarre; however, it was exactly as the community planned it to be, which was a fountain constructed and displayed to communicate the acceptance of diversity. So, while unusual, it was not out of place in Outlandish, and the people were proud of it.

Around the grand fountain was where the people met for church on Sundays, and the fashion in which they worshipped was not exactly bizarre but certainly not conventional, either. The people put their blankets out and placed their lawn chairs on the thick grass covering the ground around the fountain. It might have looked a little more like an outdoor concert. A variety of groups gathered (some large, some small), and there were always a few who, by choice, sat alone. Together the people studied their bibles, prayed, and chatted.

On this particular Sunday, the Plumbys sat alone on their oversized quilt. Elder Francis walked through the crowd of people as he wrapped up his short sermon to get ready for discussion time.

With his arms outstretched the elder spoke gently, "Romans 12 instructs us to be devoted to each other like a loving family and excel in showing respect for each other. Friends, do not be lazy in showing your devotion. Use your energy to serve the Lord. Be happy in your confidence, be patient in your trouble, and pray continually. Share what you have with God's people who are in need and be hospitable.

"Brothers and sisters, may we begin these very practices in this very moment and may those around you, as well as those throughout our entire community, feel the love of Christ through your service to them as well as your kindness."

When the elder walked away, Archie turned and said, "Father, is it wrong that I walked out on Ms. Perrelli yesterday? I don't suppose it was a gesture of kindness."

Albert put his hands on his knees and leaned forward. "Only you can answer that, son. If you were sparing her what was coming next, I would say it was definitely a gesture of kindness."

"Oh, Albert!" Annella piped in. "You know Archie wouldn't have done anything at all."

Albert chuckled. "Well, now, you never know. If he's anything like his father . . ."

"Albert!" Annella said shaking her head. "Did you not learn anything from the elder's sermon today?"

Albert only laughed.

Archie hadn't even noticed his parents' amusing exchange; instead he was still considering the situation. "Mother, I was so bothered by Ms. Perrelli. I've never met a prouder person in all my life. It seems everything she does and says is either to boast or to gain something. How do you handle people like that?"

"Archie, I know you want to be at peace with the situation, but perhaps the problem lies with

Ms. Perrelli. I doubt it has anything to do with you. I suggest you check your own heart and then let it go."

"Yes. You're right."

Albert looked around Archie's umbrella. "It looks like you're going to have to figure it out—and pretty quickly."

Archie felt instant dread. "Oh, brother," he said under his breath.

But it wasn't Gemma Perrelli's voice he first heard. It was Tallie's. "Hello, Mr. and Mrs. Plumby." Tallie bent over and ducked her head down to meet with Archie's and said a little shyly, "Hi, Archibald."

Archie stood immediately and turned around to confirm Gemma was with Tallie. He nodded and tried to smile but then focused his attention only on Tallie.

"Good afternoon, Tallie," he said, feeling his face grow warm.

Tallie scanned the area. "What is this?"

"We're having church."

"Church? Out here?"

"Yes. We meet here in Central Circle every Sunday at three."

"I've never seen a church that looks like this one," Tallie said.

Archie waited for a moment but eventually smiled and admitted, "Yes, this is probably a little different than what you're used to."

Tallie felt Gemma poke her shoulder blade and quickly said, "Oh! Ms. Perrelli wanted to find you, Archibald."

Gemma walked forward and offered a half smile. "Hello again, Archie."

Archie quickly made the decision to make peace with Gemma. "Ms. Perrelli, you've met my father."

Gemma put her hand out and said, "Yes, it's nice to see you again, Mr. Plumby."

Archie continued, "And this is my mother, Chef Annella."

Annella laughed and shook her head. "Just Annella is fine."

Gemma reached her hand out to Archie's mother and said, "Archie speaks very highly of you. I think I could learn a lot from you."

Annella looked curiously at Archie. "Hmmm. I'm not sure about that." Looking back to Ms. Perrelli she added, "It's nice to meet you."

Gemma turned her attention to Archie. "About yesterday . . . I think my words came out more bluntly than I intended. I guess it's a good thing I tell stories with photographs, yeah?"

When she followed her apology with a piercing laugh, Archie was a little irritated; however, he knew he would be required to forgive her . . . for his own peace of mind. So he took a deep breath and said, "Of course I forgive you . . . if . . . that's what . . . you're looking for."

Gemma evidently found his response a little amusing, for she smiled, but because his expression was sober, she said seriously, "Yes, Archie. I'm seeking your forgiveness."

Turning his attention back to Tallie he said, "The elder is just about to conclude the service. Would you care to stay for the parting hymn?"

"Now hymns *are* familiar," said Tallie.

Archie invited her to share his umbrella, and Gemma, feeling a little out of place at that point said, "I think I'll head back, Tallie. I'll see you at dinner?" When Gemma turned to leave, Archie remembered the elder's words: *"Show the love of Christ to others through service and through kindness."* He immediately felt bad for not inviting her to stay as well, so he turned and said, "Would you like to stay for the parting hymn, Ms. Perrelli?"

Gemma smiled but didn't turn to show it to Archie. Instead, she just lifted her hand in acknowledgment and hollered back to him, "No, thank you!"

Archie nodded as he turned back around and felt better for offering the invitation.

Before the parting hymn, the elders always took a few minutes each week to share the community's needs and upcoming events. Most often it was one of the retirees who was ill and in need of assistance and meals, but sometimes there would be a special event that needed service, a community cleanup day, or a party planned to welcome a newcomer. This week, Elder Francis said only, "Remember, next Saturday morning we are meeting to clean the fountain. The town will provide everything needed. Just have a good breakfast and come prepared to scrub. Oh . . . and just in case you need some added incentive, Pizza Garden will provide a meal for all who are still present at the lunch hour."

Tallie whispered to Archie, "That must be a pretty special fountain."

Archie laughed and said quietly, "Yes, I guess it is."

"I'm assuming there's a story there?"

"No, not really," Archie answered.

"Well, I think I'll photograph it before I leave."

Archie looked surprised. "Why would you want to do that?"

"Because it's the strangest looking fountain I've ever seen," she said, stifling a laugh.

Archie looked at Tallie. "Outlandish and you seem to get along. Are you going to stay for a while?"

"Unfortunately, only until Tuesday morning," she said a little sadly.

Archie felt a little gloomy at her news, but because he didn't want to appear as vulnerable as he felt, he only smiled and said, "I see," before turning his head back to the elder.

Tallie also carried her own bit of disappointment over having to leave so soon.

Elder Francis lifted his arms and said, "Let us sing together!"

*Now thank we all our God, with heart
and hands and voices,
Who wondrous things has done, in
whom this world rejoices;
Who from our mothers' arms has
blessed us on our way
With countless gifts of love, and still
is ours today.*

O may this bounteous God, through
all our life be near us,
With ever joyful hearts and blessed
peace to cheer us;
And keep us in His grace, and guide
us when perplexed;
And free us from all ills, in this world
and the next!

All praise and thanks to God the
Father now be given;
The Son and Him who reigns with
them in highest Heaven;
The one eternal God, whom earth and
Heaven adore;

For thus it was, is now, and shall be
evermore.

Chapter 7

It was Monday afternoon at low tide when Archie and Tallie went to the beach together to collect sea glass. Tallie had forgotten to bring along a container, so Archie offered his shirt.

"Just drop them in here," he said, holding out the bottom of his shirt.

"Are you sure?" Tallie asked. "I don't want to ruin it."

"Of course. It'll only get dirty, not ruined."

"My human bucket, huh?"

"I've been called worse things," he said with a chuckle.

Archie followed Tallie as she walked with her head down and her back bent in search of her beach treasures. He was charmed by her uninhibited enthusiasm and hoped she wouldn't soon find him boring for his steady and undemanding demeanor.

"What's this?" she asked, walking toward him with something in her hand.

"It appears to be . . . a rock."

She laughed. "Well, at least it's a pretty one!"

"Do you want to keep it?" he asked.

"No, that's okay," she said taking one last look and throwing it in the waves.

Tallie turned and walked away to continue her search. Archie knew she saw something when she began to run. Turning toward Archie she shouted, "Archibald, I think it's sea glass!"

Just as she was about to grab it up, an old man who was standing nearby picked it up, stuffed it in his pocket without even inspecting it, and turned to walk away. Tallie gasped, "Did you see that? He didn't even look at me!"

"I'm sorry. Collectors can be pretty ruthless."

"Sheesh. I guess."

Archie gave her a sympathetic look. "Why don't we go and look by the rocks?"

Tallie shrugged and seemed discouraged. "Look at all the people over there. I'll bet they've already taken everything."

"You never know until you look for your-self," he said.

Archie and his umbrella leaned against a rock and waited as Tallie searched. He was entertained by the excitement she expressed over each little item found. When she seemed to be content with her finds, she finally walked up to Archie and waited for him to hold out his shirt.

Dropping the items in, she said, "Can we move a little closer to the water?"

"You go ahead," he said. "I'll wait here."

"Are you sure? You're not getting bored, are you?"

"Not at all," he said.

"Okay. I'll be right back!" she said before running off.

What he didn't tell Tallie was that he'd stumbled over the rocks a few times and since both hands were occupied at present, he didn't want to run the risk of creating a scene.

The wind was blowing lightly, as it often did, and Tallie seemed to be annoyed at the way her hair kept blowing into her face, but Archie was amused at the way she continually pushed it away and pulled it out of her mouth. In fact, he was so distracted by it that he failed to notice the wave coming in behind her, so without a warning, it crashed against her while she was still bent over. Archie jolted away from the rock, dropping everything that was in his shirt and ran toward her.

She laughed as she continued running away from the water. Archie moved toward her and grabbed her hand as soon as he could. Together they ran away from the water. When they were at a safe distance from the waves, they laughed together under Archie's umbrella.

"Oh boy!" she said, looking down at her wet clothes.

"You don't visit the beach much, do you?" he asked.

"How'd you guess?"

"May I give you a piece of advice?"

"I'm listening," she said.

"Never turn your back to the water."

"Lesson learned!" she said, laughing and squeezing the water from her hair. "But it was worth it! Look what I found!"

Tallie opened her hand and held out a little piece of pink sea glass.

"Didn't you say pink is one of the hardest to find?"

"Yes, it is," he said. "I'm surprised you held onto it when the wave hit."

"Me, too!"

Tallie started to put her glass in his shirt. "Oh. Where . . . ?"

"Oh no. When I ran to rescue you, I must have dropped everything."

"Rescue me?" she laughed.

He turned to look back where he was standing and saw the little pile he had dropped.

"It looks like everything is safe, though."

Tallie ran over and sat in the sand to look at everything she'd gathered.

Archie knew immediately it was a bad decision. "You do realize you just sat a very wet you down in the dry sand?"

Tallie stood quickly and soon realized her mistake. "Oh, I didn't think of that" she said with a sigh. "Is that rule number two?"

"Evidently," he said. "Portland isn't so far from the beach. Why haven't you been more often?"

"I only moved to Portland when my mom was diagnosed with cancer two years ago. She was having treatment there. I'm originally from Kansas City. I don't have much experience with coastal living."

"Ah! It all makes sense now. Well, I was going to ask you to go for tea, but maybe you'll want to change first?"

"Oh, that's okay. I have to meet Gemma for dinner, so I don't have much time. Why don't we just hang out while I dry off, and then I'll go and get ready for dinner? That is if you won't be embarrassed being with me," she said looking down at her wet clothes.

Archie shook his head. "Impossible. Why don't we go to my place? We can have our tea on the porch and the sun can dry you."

"That sounds perfect."

While having tea, Archie and Tallie talked and laughed and spent those hours feeling like they'd known each other much longer than they had.

When it was time for Tallie to leave, Archie said, "I'd like to see you off tomorrow if you don't mind. What time are you leaving?"

"Around nine, I think."

"Would it be all right if I met you at The Lupine a little before nine?"

"Sure!" Putting her hand on Archie's arm, Tallie said, "I had a lot of fun today, Archibald."

He glanced down at her hand on his arm. "So did I, Tallie."

"Well, I better run." She turned to leave and hollered back, "I guess I'll see you tomorrow!"

On Tuesday morning, Archie met Tallie at The Lupine. Holding up a brown bag he said, "I brought you some of my mother's pastries."

Looking inside the bag she squealed, "The orange cheesecake ones!"

"Indeed," said Archie, chuckling. "I'd be more than happy to tell you what they're really called."

"I guess you'd better," she said laughing.

"Are you ready for this?" asked Archie in a teasing voice.

Tallie opened her eyes widely and nodded exaggeratedly.

"Orange . . . Cheese . . . Pastries."

Showing mock disappointment, Tallie said, "That's *it*?"

"Yes. Direct and to the point though. Don't you think?"

Tallie said, "If it were my job to give them a name, I would name them . . ." Looking up at the sky while she considered the perfect words she said slowly, "Luscious . . . Cheesy . . . Orange . . . Happiness!"

Archie laughed. "Very clever. I'll let Mother know. She might be willing to change the name."

Because they were laughing, they didn't see Gemma Perrelli walk out the door of The Lupine.

"Oh, hi Archie," Gemma said casually.

Archie and Tallie both startled, but then Archie said, "Good morning."

Gemma set her suitcase down and asked, "Will you watch this for me, Tallie? I think I dropped my lens cap somewhere."

When Gemma walked back inside, Archie said, rolling his eyes, "Well, that's a relief."

She slapped his arm playfully. "Archibald!"

"Well, it is."

"You're funny."

"You think so?" he asked, truly curious.

"Well, you make *me* laugh."

Only a few people had ever considered Archie funny (at least as far as he knew) and those were his mother, his father and his lifelong friend, Luke. He knew that was because those were the people he was most comfortable around and could be completely himself with.

He reached out and touched Tallie's cheek with the back of his hand. "I'm so happy we met, Tallie."

Feeling he might have been a little too forward, he quickly pulled his hand away. Tallie felt her neck and face grow warm, and wondered if she was getting splotchy, but she enjoyed Archie's show of affection so decided not to worry about it.

"So am I, Archibald. I *am* sad about not getting any photos of you, though. The time went by too fast."

Archie surprised himself by lifting his hand once again and placing it against her upper arm.

"Well then, you'll just have to come back to get your pictures."

"I will," she answered.

"When?"

"I don't know, but I promise I will."

He lowered his hand from her arm. "Mind if I write to you?"

"I'd love it!" said Tallie. "Or you could call."

Archie said, "I'm afraid I'm not much for talking on the phone."

"Oh, okay," she said. "Why?"

"I'm not quite sure . . . but I *can* dance," he said.

Tallie laughed. "Can you really ... or is that a joke?"

"No, I really can. I love dancing, at least with Mother . . . in our living room. I thought it might be a good time to bring it up since . . . well, since I don't talk on the phone. You know how some people don't dance? Well, I do . . . but I don't talk on the phone. See the humor in that?"

"Totally," Tallie said with an exaggerated nod. "Yeah, I get it. See how funny you are?"

Tallie put her head down and started digging in her purse. She pulled out a little notebook and quickly wrote down her address as well as her phone number. "I put my number there just in case you get brave and decide to call me."

Archie took the paper and put it in his pocket. "Not likely, but I will write to you."

"And I'll write back." Tallie surprised Archie by moving forward, standing on her toes, and kissing him on the cheek. When she stepped back, he reached out with his free hand and took her hand into his.

"Thank you for spending time with me while you were here."

Tallie kept ahold of Archie's hand and used her other arm to hug him around the neck—the umbrella shaft between them.

She whispered to him, "I've never met anyone quite like you, Archibald." Stepping back, she added, "I'll think of you every time I admire my sea glass."

Archie smiled crookedly.

Tallie continued. "And keep writing those children's stories. You're talented. I really think you could get your work published."

Archie took Tallie's words to heart. "We'll see. I wouldn't even know where to start."

"Maybe you could start by contacting some agents? I mean, I don't know anything about publishing, but I'll bet an agent could really help."

"Perhaps," said Archie with a shrug.

"Promise me you'll give it some thought?"

Archie nodded and smiled at Tallie. "I appreciate your confidence in my writing. It does provoke some courage."

Without Archie or Tallie realizing, Gemma had walked back outside. When she saw them holding hands under the umbrella, she couldn't resist lifting her camera and quickly snapping a photo of the two of them.

Archie heard the click of the camera and looked up to see Gemma putting the lens cap on. He quickly let go of Tallie's hand and stepped back.

"Um, I guess I should be getting back," he said. "I hope you have a nice trip home."

He was speaking to Tallie, but it was Gemma who responded. "It was nice meeting you, Archie."

"Yes. You, too, Ms. Perrelli. Tallie, safe travels."

With that, Archie and his umbrella turned to leave.

Tallie watched Archie until she could no longer see him. Suddenly she turned to Gemma. "Would you mind if I ran a quick errand before we left?"

"No, that's all right. I need to make a couple of phone calls. I'll get a cup of coffee and meet you back here in, say, half an hour?"

"Yes, that would be great! Thanks!" she said before rushing off.

Tallie thought Archie might have gone to the beach. She thought she might follow him there and get photographs of him before she left. She knew she would have to catch him unaware or the photos would never be successful.

She walked by his house and scanned the beach to see if he was there. He was. It was early and the beach was still fairly deserted. She saw some runners along the path as well as a few collectors here and there, but where Archie stood, he was alone staring out at the water.

Tallie walked down the wooden stairs, pulled her telephoto lens out of her bag, and snapped a few pictures. What she couldn't observe from her view was the prayer Archie was directing upward. "Lord, I'm about to ask you something I've never asked before. It's caught me quite off guard, and I'll admit I feel a little confused by it all, but do you think you could send Tallie back to me?"

When Tallie felt satisfied she'd taken enough pictures, she smiled, mouthed the words, "I'll miss you," and turned and walked back to Central Circle to meet Gemma Perrelli.

Chapter 8

Archie wasn't at all himself. It had been two weeks since Tallie had gone back home and not only did his days feel long, but his routine seemed tedious and even boring. He had tried to write to Tallie but everything he wrote seemed either too presumptuous or too general. He tried to write for his column as well, but that meant he had to observe what was going on around him, and being distracted by his own thoughts made the task extraordinarily difficult. It was a good thing he had a stash of writings he hadn't yet submitted to the paper. They gave him something to fall back on until he could clear his mind.

It was three o'clock in the afternoon, and Archie would normally be writing, but instead he was lying on his bed, deep in thought.

"Archie!"

It was his mother's voice, and he could tell she was coming up the stairs. He quickly got off of his bed and grabbed his notebook so his mother wouldn't suspect anything. She knocked on the door, and Archie answered as casually as he could. "Uh, come in."

Rather than entering his room, his mother just opened the door and bent down to hand him a letter. "Look what came for you!" she said in a singsongy voice.

Archie moved over to the door and took the letter from his mother's hand. When he saw it was from Tallie, he looked up in confusion.

"Well," she said, "don't look so surprised."

"I *am* surprised though. I haven't written to her, and I didn't give her our address."

"Well, Archie, she didn't have to be a genius to figure that one out."

"I guess you're right."

"Of course, I'm right," she said with a chuckle. "I'm off to work. Your father is traveling tonight, so would you mind, very much, coming to the restaurant for dinner?"

"No, not at all. I'll come by later."

Archie's mother blew him a kiss. "Enjoy your afternoon . . . *and* your letter," she teased as she walked away.

When his mother walked out, Archie pushed the door shut and sat against it. He turned the envelope over in his hands and tried to guess what it might say before opening it. When curiosity finally won, he opened the envelope carefully.

Dear Archibald,
You haven't written to me! I really hoped you would. I hope it's okay that I decided to write to you.

I had such a great time when I was in Outlandish and I really miss spending time with you, but I've been keeping busy with Ms. Perrelli.

Since she didn't really make any connections last time we were there, she mentioned going back to Outlandish. Of course, that's great with me, as long as I get to go with her.

I'm enjoying my beach treasures. I keep them in a box, and as promised, I think of you when I'm admiring them. I've even photographed them (although the photographs aren't nearly as pretty as the real thing).

I'm not sure why, but Ms. Perrelli decided to teach me close-up photography, and I mean really close up. It's called macro photography and requires a special lens (which I bought, even though it was more money than I'm used to spending on lenses). Since she's my teacher, I justified it by calling it an investment in my future. That makes sense, right?

We went to a Japanese garden in Portland to get our photos. I've always liked flowers, but have never taken time to learn the names of most of them. Ms. Perrelli, however, knew the names of all of them. I couldn't believe it! I asked her if there was anything she didn't know, and she just laughed. Really, though, I was impressed.

Just looking through the lens was an experience. You wouldn't believe how different things look that close up. I'm not very good at it yet, but you should see her photographs. They are stunning, and I'm very excited to learn more. It's like having a completely different view of life.

I guess that's enough about me. I'm looking forward to hearing back from you. I hope you have been busy writing stories and that you are seriously considering what I said. I really think you could be famous. I know you're laughing right now, aren't you? But one of these days I'm sure you'll be thanking me for helping you discover your destiny.

I'll wrap this up. I'm off to dinner with Patrice. We've both been missing Mom, so we decided we needed some time out to rehash some good memories. We're eating at Upmarket Donuts. I know it sounds like a weird choice for dinner, but these aren't your typical donuts. Last time I ate there I had a ham and Swiss. Tonight I think I'll try their macaroni-and-cheese donut topped with bacon. I've heard they're delicious. (Don't tell your mother about my dinner choices. She probably wouldn't understand.)

I hope you'll write back and let me know how you are and how the writing is going.

Thinking of you,
Tallie

Archie was smiling when he folded the letter and put it back inside the envelope. He moved over to his shelf and found a piece of paper and a pen. He now felt he knew what would be appropriate to write, so it took him no time at all to formulate a two-page letter. He felt anxious to get it in the mail, so he addressed and stamped it and decided to walk it to the post office.

On the way, he heard from behind, "How'd you manage to make the front page, Arch?"

Archie turned around, knowing it was his friend Luke. Luke was almost as tall as Archie and even a little more slender. The thing everyone noticed first on Luke was his wide smile. After that, you would see his suspenders over his white button-up shirt, along with his black porkpie hat worn on top of shoulder-length black hair.

Archie walked toward him and put out his hand. "Luke. How are you?"

Luke was holding a newspaper in his hand and said with a chuckle, "Apparently not as well as you, brother."

Archie tilted his head and narrowed his eyes. "What do you mean?"

Luke held up the newspaper that was folded in half. On the front page was a photo of Archie and Tallie underneath his umbrella.

"What's this?" asked Archie.

Luke showed Archie the other side of the folded paper.

"The Pacific Coast Buzz! What? How?" Putting out his hand, Archie asked, "May I?"

Luke handed him the paper and said, "Sorry, Arch. I assumed you knew. What's up?"

Archie shook his head and read out loud, *"Ten Ways to Romance Your Lady by Eagen Finney.* Who's Eagen Finney?"

Luke shrugged his shoulders. "Never heard of him."

Archie took a few minutes to scan the article and was grateful to discover there wasn't any mention of him or Tallie, and that the photo was only a prop, but he was still unhappy about it and knew exactly who was behind it. Underneath it read: PHOTO CREDIT: GEMMA PERRELLI.

"Is everything all right, bro?" Luke asked.

"Yes, yes. Fine. Sorry. I just—"

Before Archie could finish, Luke put up his hands and said, "Hey, it's none of my business . . . but who's the girl, Arch?"

Archie said as casually as he could, "Oh, she's, um, just an acquaintance."

Laughing at Archie's choice of words, Luke said, "Just an acquaintance? Mm-hm."

Archie dropped his head to the side and offered a one-sided smile. After that, he changed the subject. "How's the magic business treating you, Luke?"

Willing to let the conversation change directions, Luke responded with, "Good. We've had some decent crowds."

"I've noticed," said Archie. "And summer hasn't even arrived. Just wait till the vacationers come."

"Summer's definitely the moneymaking season for us," said Luke.

"How's Lily?" asked Archie. "Have you set a date yet for the wedding?"

"Yeah, we did, but . . ."

When Luke didn't finish, Archie cocked his head. "But what?"

Luke looked away from Archie. "Arch, she changed her mind."

"Changed her mind? About marrying you?"

Luke looked back at Archie, pressed his lips together, and nodded.

Archie put his hand on Luke's shoulder. "Ah Luke, I'm sorry. When did this happen?"

"About a week ago."

"Why didn't you tell me sooner?" Archie asked.

Luke shook his head. "I haven't been coping very well, Arch. I thought if I just hid away for a while, I might eventually get a grip, you know?" Archie felt a great deal of compassion for his longtime friend and responded with an uncharacteristic one-armed hug. While he had Luke there he said, "I don't know what I can do, but I'm here for you, all right?"

Luke didn't answer, but Archie felt him acknowledge his words with a nod. He patted him affectionately on the back and backed away. Luke turned his head away again and Archie knew he was trying to pull himself together.

"Why don't we go for coffee?" Archie suggested.

"I'd love to, Arch, but I'm pretty sure I'm late for rehearsal."

Archie laughed. "Luke Pindabrook late for rehearsal? No! That can't be."

Luke sneered at Archie. "What?"

They both laughed. Archie hit Luke on the arm and said, "Take care of yourself, Luke. Let's get together soon."

Archie began his walk toward home, but quickly remembered the letter. He pulled it out of his pocket, held it up in front of his face, and said under his breath, "Archibald, you've lost your mind."

He turned back toward the post office but decided he would like to add the photograph from the paper to his letter. So instead of mailing the letter, he went to buy two papers. One to keep and the other to send to Tallie.

A part of him wanted Tallie to have the photo so she could remember their time together, but another part of him wanted to send it with a note scolding Gemma Perrelli. He decided it would serve both purposes.

Once home, he cut out the photo and stared at it for a while. In the photo his umbrella was slightly slanted and hiding most of his head. You could only see his face below his eyes, and Tallie could only be seen from the side. It *was* a charming photo. He could see how nicely it fit as a prop for the article, but he couldn't help but feel violated and a little cross.

He carefully opened the sealed envelope and removed the letter. He sat down and added a postscript.

> P.S. Evidently Ms. Perrelli snapped a photo of us in the moments before our parting. I was surprised when a friend of mine brought it to my attention by showing me the article it was placed with, in the PC Buzz. I understand she's a photographer and snapping photos comes easily for her, but please remind Ms. Perrelli that I declined her offer to be photographed, and I hope she will respect my wishes in the future. I'm sure her boldness benefits her in her career, but I'm pretty sure it makes her few friends. (Don't tell her that part.)

When he was finished, he folded the letter around the photo, put it back into the envelope and used a little glue to reseal it. After that, he walked it back to the post office and dropped the letter in the box.

Chapter 9

When the sun was up, Archie usually was, too, but on this day four weeks after Tallie's departure he was still in bed staring up at his close white canopy. He rubbed his eyes with his palms and left his fingers resting in the clump of hair on his forehead.

He had hoped time would naturally rekindle his desire to write and to carry on as usual, but when he awoke that morning, he felt certain it would be another day of the same struggles. He scolded himself, "Good grief Archibald! It would be totally pathetic to lose such a little job."

He lifted his hands into the air as if surrendering to fate.

If any of you lacks wisdom, you should ask God, who gives generously.

The words came to him without any effort at all . . . and when they did, Archie felt a great sense of guilt. He had always been one to pray about things, but in the midst of boredom and a preoccupied mind, he'd forgotten to.

"Of course!" he said out loud.

Rolling out of bed, he got on his knees, and prayed.

God didn't always answer Archie's prayers the way he desired, but He did always answer his prayers, and that knowledge gave him the courage to hope for some insight in the days ahead.

It was the morning after Archie's prayer that he woke up with a new resolve. Although he was the type who thrived on routine, on this morning, he wondered if God might be telling him to keep an open mind—to be willing to move away from his routine and explore life a bit more. He usually spoke to his mother about issues of the heart, but since this was something a little different, he decided to talk to his father.

It was early evening when Archie approached his father. Albert was in his usual chair, smoking his favorite pipe, drinking his evening tea, and reading the newspaper.

"May I talk to you, Father?"

Albert looked up from his paper. "Of course."

Archie grabbed an umbrella stand and moved to the chair opposite his father. He sat down, placed his umbrella in the stand, and adjusted it until it was positioned correctly. When he looked at his father, he realized he had his full attention.

"I think I have a problem," Archie said.

His father remained quiet while Archie tried to choose the best words to express his dilemma.

"You remember Tallie?"

"Of course I remember Tallie," his father said with a chuckle.

"Well, since she left, I haven't been myself. I assume I have feelings for her, but it's changed me . . . in unexpected ways. I can't seem to figure it out."

Archie's father smiled. "That's no surprise. She took a bit of your heart with her, didn't she?"

"Has it been that obvious?" he asked, feeling a little embarrassed.

"Yes," Archie's father said with a grin. "Your mother and I have had a few conversations about it, but we didn't want to make you uncomfortable, so we decided we'd wait until you came to us."

Feeling a little self-conscious, Archie put his head down and scratched his cheek.

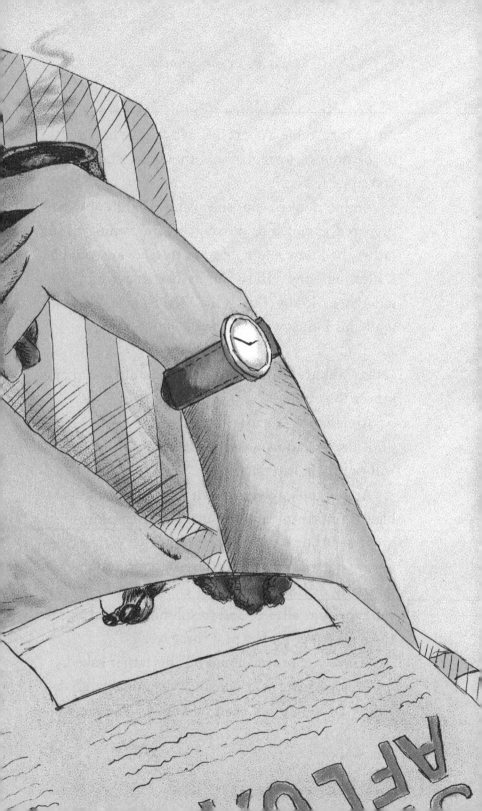

Knowing it was going to be an awkward conversation for Archie, Albert decided to give him a little bit of time to formulate his thoughts. "Let me fix you some tea."

Archie looked up sheepishly. While he had prepared as much as possible before coming to his father, he knew a few minutes to recover would be a blessing—and clearly his father knew him well enough to know that, too. "Thank you," he said while his father walked away.

"Here you are," his father said, handing a cup and saucer to Archie.

Archie took the tea. "Thank you."

Albert sat down and leaned back in his chair. "All right. I'm listening."

Archie took a deep breath through his nose and blew it out through his mouth before speaking.

"I seem to be so distracted lately. Writing has always been such an effortless activity. It comes as naturally as breathing, but I can't seem to do it. I can't focus at all. I've had to submit old writings to the newspaper for the past three weeks."

"Have you prayed about it?" his father asked.

"Yes," Archie said quickly, but immediately felt guilty. Dropping his head he added, "Although I'll admit to waiting until yesterday. I've just been so out of sorts."

"And what has God said to you since your prayer?" his father asked.

"Not much yet, but He did make two things clear."

"And what were they?" asked his father.

"I believe God is asking me to keep an open mind." Archie sighed. "We both know that isn't my strong suit."

Albert chuckled. "It sounds like you must *make* it your strong suit."

"Yes," Archie said, nodding. "The only other thing I knew to do was to come and talk to you. I'm willing to adjust my life . . . I think. I'm just not sure how that will settle my mind. Maybe I could change up my routine a little, maybe get up a little earlier . . . eat something different for breakfast . . . or, I don't know, look for some more work?"

Albert almost laughed, but Archie was so serious, he made great effort to resist by putting his head down, covering his mouth with his hand and clearing his throat. Lifting his chin, his father said seriously, "This isn't just about changing your routine or even looking for a new job. It's about following your instincts and seeking what is already waiting for you. You seem to have reached a plateau, son. I think there's more for you out there."

"More of what? Please, give me the exact steps to take, Father."

Albert looked up as if trying to pull the right words out of the air. "Do you know how I met your mother, Archie?"

"Yes, you were traveling on business in England, right?"

"Mm-hm, that's right, but I've never told you the circumstances that led me there." His father continued. "Like you, Archie, I was always a good student. I loved studying and learning about things, so when I graduated high school, it was a natural next step to continue my education and earn a degree. The problem was, I had done well in all of my classes, but I wasn't sure what I wanted to pursue as a career. I had no specific interests. I was tested and counseled and based on my academic strengths, I chose a degree in finance.

"Four years later, I graduated with my bachelor's degree, and I was offered a position as a loan officer at a large bank. It was a steady, good paying job, and I liked it for a while, but after only a few months, my work became dull and the days were horribly long. By the time I got home each day, I had so little energy I would put a frozen meal in the oven, eat in front of the television, and fall asleep on the sofa."

Archie furrowed his brow. "That sounds nothing like you. You're the most enterprising man I've ever known."

"Thank you, Archie. That's not always been the case, however, which is why I brought it up."

"What changed?" Archie asked.

"It was a poster."

"A poster?"

"Yes, I was at the market buying my frozen dinners and I saw a poster on the wall by the restrooms. For whatever reason, it caught my attention."

Archie looked at his father and nodded once, encouraging him to go on.

"The poster said this: 'Don't let a day go by without reaching for something you love.' When I looked closer I saw it was an advertisement for a local bakery with pictures of pastries and doughnuts. I suppose it's likely the pastries are what caught my attention in the first place. I've always had such a ridiculous sweet tooth."

Archie shook his head. "It spoke to you because you weren't doing what you loved."

"Yes, son. That's exactly what it was."

"So what did you do?"

"Well, I kept my job at first, but I set out to see and do everything I could. I went to every local event: art galleries, festivals, wine tastings, ballets, garden shows, parades . . . you name it, I was there. Instead of going with friends, which in my case would have created a crutch, I went to all the events alone. I wanted God to bring new people into my life. I wanted Him to direct my next steps. That's exactly what He did, too. I met so many lively, interesting people."

"And what doors opened for you?"

Albert laughed. "All of them! Well, at least enough for me to glance inside. Those experiences brought me back to life. I started inventing business ideas and planning my own ventures. I wasn't sure where to begin, so I started with something small I could do on weekends, still keeping my job at the bank."

"What did you do?" asked Archie.

"You'd never guess," Albert answered.

"What was it?"

"I bought a little freezer cart and sold frozen grapes at nearby events."

"Grapes? Really?" Archie asked surprised.

Albert continued. "It didn't matter what event I attended, I noticed the lines at the beverage vendors were always long. People get thirsty when they're frolicking about, I suppose. So I tried to think of something I could sell that would quench thirst but wasn't a drink at all.

"I experimented with freezing a variety of fruits to see which one was the least messy, the easiest to eat frozen, and most importantly, the most delicious. The grapes won.

"I hired a painter to decorate my cart. I bought red, purple, and green grapes. I froze them at home and stored them in containers in my freezer, and on event days, I transferred them to my cart and sold them by the cupful. They were a great hit! I always sold out within just a few hours."

"Grapes! You're right, I never would've guessed."

"Yes, well, believe it or not, that business allowed me to quit my job at the bank. The money wasn't nearly as good, but I was a much happier man. When I was ready to move on, I sold my cart and that was that.

"I had many other start-ups and successes and sold a variety of small businesses. Eventually I knew what I was meant to do. I was a man of ideas, and I enjoyed the adrenaline rush of taking risks. I was meant to be an entrepreneur."

Archie shook his head and sighed. "That's quite inspiring. But I still don't know how you met Mother. What business were you on in England?"

Albert lifted his head. "Ohhhh yes, England. When I had been on my own for three years, I decided I was ready to learn more. I wanted to see other places and explore other cultures. My first overseas visit would be to England.

"While I was there, I went to the Old Queens Head pub in Sheffield . . . to learn more about beer, you know."

At this, Archie laughed. "Father, really."

Albert laughed as well. "All right, so I wasn't really there to learn about beer, but I did buy myself one . . . or two. Ha! When I was on my way out, I spotted your mother and decided she was the most beautiful thing I'd ever laid eyes on.

"She was wearing a knee-length dress as well as a floppy straw hat with a green ribbon around it. She was carrying a watering can and was walking from pot to pot along the street. She was caring for the flowers."

"Your memory is brilliant," Archie interjected.

"Your mother was brilliant."

"Did you introduce yourself?" Archie asked.

"Of course, I did! I wasn't going to let her get away. She was shy about going to dinner. She was only seventeen, and I was twenty-five. So I looked for her every day and talked to her until finally, after a week or so, she agreed to have dinner with me. Love came rather quickly after that.

"You see, Archie, I never would have met your mother if I'd stayed at my dull job at the bank. When I reached that plateau, it was my responsibility to respond by venturing out . . . reaching a little higher. That's what you're ready for, Archie."

Archie closed his eyes and breathed in deeply, lifting his chest high. When he opened his eyes, he blew out a quick breath. "So I guess . . . I start climbing, looking around every corner," he said matter-of-factly, "and see what happens."

"Precisely," his father answered.

"But you don't think I'll have to stop writing, do you? Writing *is* what I love. I can't imagine life without it."

"Archie, if writing is what you love, well then, writing is what you *must* do. Let your passion for it drive you. It will take you where you need to go. If there is more for you in the way of writing . . . go and find it!"

Archie's posture had gone from rigid to relaxed. "This conversation is just what I needed," he said with a sigh. "I feel very inspired."

Albert stood and motioned for Archie to stand as well. Archie lifted his umbrella off of the stand and stood up with it.

"I love you, Son," he said before wrapping both arms around Archie, "and aren't we lucky your mother is a chef? No frozen dinners for us!"

Archie shook his head, smiled, and said, "No. Thank goodness for that."

Chapter 10

Archie's perspective changed after his conversation with his father, and while he still thought of Tallie, almost every hour, he was no longer so distracted by those thoughts that he was unable to function.

His plan was to do what his father had done, which was to search everywhere for the unknown something that might be waiting just around the corner; and while it was a bit frightening for Archie, it was, at the same time, exhilarating.

Just as his father had done, Archie retained his job at *Stay Afloat* and continued to submit articles, although he did supplement them occasionally with his previously written works. Archie's plan was to spend at least three hours each day exploring his mind, his town, his heart, and his prospects. He walked through Outlandish, intentionally and thoroughly, inspecting everything. He went in and out of shops, walked by every food cart, read every new sign and poster that hung here and there, and struck up conversation with as many people as seemed willing—and that part wasn't at all easy for Archie.

Archie read two newspapers: *Stay Afloat*, which was only distributed on Tuesdays and Saturdays, and the *Pacific Coast Buzz*, which was distributed daily. He always took them to Outlandish's library to read and made himself scan every single page of each newspaper including the classifieds.

Quaint libraries in very small towns never seem to be quite busy and neither was the one in Outlandish; that is why Archie loved spending time there. This library was especially narrow and oddly high. There was a spiral staircase going up, and as much as it didn't quite fit, there was also an elevator crammed into the small building. Each level of books could be seen from the first floor and each of those levels was an exact replica of the one below it. While there wasn't a lot of room to roam, there were plenty of books to choose from. They stood on shelves, which rose all the way to the short ceilings on each level, and rolling ladders made each one of them accessible.

This had always been a place where Archie could go for as long as he liked and no one would ever bother him, even though his umbrella did take up an unreasonable amount of space in the cramped quarters.

Children in Outlandish were scarce, so the large number of children's books in the library was a bit excessive, but the aged librarian, Mrs. Pinkers, had once owned a children's bookstore in Delaware and was terribly tempted by all the beautiful covers on the children's books. She spent much too much of her book budget on what would only be read by a few, but nobody ever protested, so she continued to indulge.

The librarian had been around long enough to know Archie was quite fond of the children's books, so she made sure he knew about each new book that came. Often she'd even ask for his help in choosing which ones to purchase from the catalogs.

It was Friday, just after breakfast, when Archie walked into the library with his newspaper.

"Good morning, Archibald!" called Mrs. Pinkers from behind the front desk. Mrs. Pinkers had always called Archie by his given name, because it was her father's name and she was especially fond of it.

"Good morning, Mrs. Pinkers," Archie said smiling.

"Oh Archibald, you just have to see this beautiful new book that came in this morning."

Mrs. Pinkers walked around the desk and held out the book in front of Archie. As she handed it to him, she smoothed the cover with her hand as if presenting a rare piece of artwork.

Archie read the cover, *When Someone Smiles.*

"May I?" he asked, pointing at the table.

"Of course," answered Mrs. Pinkers.

Mrs. Pinkers walked back to the front desk, and Archie walked over to the table and extended his portable umbrella stand. After putting his umbrella into it and adjusting it, he began reading.

Mrs. Pinkers watched from the desk in anticipation because she loved discussing the stories with Archie. But then the phone rang. Mrs. Pinkers sighed before she went to the back room to answer.

"Hello," came a small voice next to Archie.

Thinking he was alone, Archie startled and looked in the direction of the voice. He was surprised to see a little girl standing next to him with a smile on her face. Archie thought she was cute with her tight blond curls and brown freckles, but he did wonder why she was there.

"Hello," answered Archie while quickly scanning the library. "And . . . who might you be?"

"Felicity," she answered. "What's your name?"

Archie looked around for her parents but didn't see anyone, not even Mrs. Pinkers.

"I'm Archibald. Where are your parents?"

"At home," she answered.

Knowing he'd never seen her in Outlandish, he asked, "And where is home?"

"Over there," she said pointing out the window.

"I think you might be a little young to be here alone. How old are you, five, maybe six?"

She didn't answer but instead asked, "Why do you have an umbrella?"

Archie looked up and said, "It's a little difficult to explain."

Felicity didn't respond but only stood waiting for an answer.

Archie said, "Are you frightened of anything, Felicity?"

Felicity shrugged and said, "Some things."

"Well, I'm a little frightened by looking up at open spaces."

When Felicity didn't seem to understand, he clarified for her. "I have my umbrella so that my ceiling is lowered. Otherwise I don't cope so well."

Felicity looked up at the ceiling and said, "This is a very high ceiling."

"It certainly is. But even a short ceiling is too high for me to look at." Archie looked for Mrs. Pinkers, but he still didn't see her. "You aren't here alone, are you?"

Felicity giggled. "No, I'm here with you, silly."

"Well, that is true, but what if I were a scary man?" Archie said, making his eyes look a little wild.

Felicity laughed and said, "You're not scary, Mr. Archibald."

Archie was tickled at how she addressed him and said, "No, I'm not very scary, am I?"

Felicity shook her head and asked, "What are you reading?"

Archie pushed the book toward her.

"Will you read it to me?" she asked, pushing the book back.

"Oh. Well."

"Pleeeeease."

"You . . . want me . . . to read it, to you?"

Felicity nodded.

Archie scanned the room for Mrs. Pinkers one last time. Reading to children certainly wasn't something he was used to, but Archie couldn't think of a good reason to say no, and he was trying to do things out of the ordinary, so instead he said, "Well, I suppose I could . . . read it to you."

Felicity pushed a chair next to Archie's so that it sat right next to him under his umbrella, then she climbed up onto it. Before opening the book, Archie said, "*When Someone Smiles* by Penelope King."

When he opened the cover, Felicity looked at him and offered a reassuring smile. Archie began reading.

When someone smiles,
the world begins to change.

To the sad, a smile says—
Joy will return.

To the cheerful, a smile says—
I share in your happiness.

To the cross, a smile says—
Please soften your heart.

To the caring, a smile says—
Thank you.

To the lost, a smile says—
I'll help.

To the hard at work, a smile says—
Well done.

To the troubled, a smile says—
There's hope.

To the one celebrating, a smile says—
Congratulations!

To the fearful, a smile says—
Have courage.

To the traveler, a smile says—
Bon voyage!

To the worried, a smile says—
Be comforted.

To the adventurer, a smile says—
You're brave.

To the weary, a smile says—
Rest yourself.

When someone smiles,
the world begins to change.

When you smile,
you change the world.

Archie shut the book and put it face-up on the table. He sat quietly for a moment not quite knowing what to say. Felicity surprised him by hugging his arm and saying, "Thank you, Mr. Archibald."

Archie patted her on the head. "You're quite welcome. And how did you like the story?"

"I liked it," she said, smiling widely.

Archie chuckled. "Yes, so did I. Shall we change the world then?"

Felicity nodded excitedly, scooted off of her chair, and happily ran off.

"Wait, where are you going?" Archie called after her.

Felicity turned and said, "To see Great Grammie."

Archie watched her run to Mrs. Pinkers who was now putting books on the shelf. Raising his hands in the air he said quietly, "Now how did I miss that?"

Mrs. Pinkers hugged her great-granddaughter and said, "How did you like the story, sweetie?"

"I liked it a lot, Great Grammie."

"Oh, good! Now why don't you go to the back and eat that snack we brought for you?"

Felicity waved at Archie. "Bye, Mr. Archibald!"

Archie waved back and smiled. Mrs. Pinkers walked over to Archie and sat down. Mrs. Pinkers winked at Archie with her wrinkled eyes. "It seems you've won a little girl's heart ... *Mr. Archibald.*"

Archie dropped his head and put his hands up. "What can I say?"

"And what did *you* think of the story, Archibald? Are you as impressed with it as I am?"

Archie smiled and said, "Yes. Yes, I liked it. The illustrations were done beautifully and the story was ... well, clever ... and even, *inspiring.*"

"I thought so, too!" said Mrs. Pinkers.

Archie's smile grew.

Mrs. Pinkers asked, "What?"

"Oh, it's nothing," Archie said, trying to put his smile aside.

"You know I'm a good listener," said Mrs. Pinkers.

"Yes, well, it's just I had a little revelation, that's all."

"From the smile on your face, it appears it was a good one."

Archie laughed through his nose. "Yes, it was a good one."

Archie looked fondly at Mrs. Pinkers. "Thank you, Mrs. Pinkers."

"For what, Archibald?"

"For being an inspiration all these years."

Mrs. Pinkers patted Archie's arm. "Well, I'm not sure how I did it, but . . . you're welcome."

Archie folded up his papers, so Mrs. Pinkers asked, "Leaving so soon?"

"Yes, I just realized there's something I need to take care of."

When Archie lifted his umbrella out of its stand, Mrs. Pinkers stood and said, "I suppose I better get back to work. Will you tell your parents hello for me?"

"I certainly will," was Archie's answer.

"Children's stories," Archie announced to his parents almost as soon as he walked in the front door. "I think God wants me to write for children."

Albert walked up to Archie. "Did you see your poster, Son?"

It only took Archie a moment to realize what his father was asking. He smiled and with a nod, answered, "Yes, Father. I saw my poster."

Chapter 11

Annella was shopping at the market when she saw Tallie walk through the door.

"Tallie! What are you doing here?" Annella hollered while walking over to her with a bundle of scallions in her hand. "Archie didn't tell me you were coming."

Tallie gave Annella a hug then stepped back. "Oh, well, he didn't know. It was last minute. I didn't have time to write to him."

Annella smiled. "Well, he'll be delighted to see you again. It's been a few months now, hasn't it?"

"Yes, it has," said Tallie. "We've written a little, but I've been so busy with Ms. Perrelli I haven't had a lot of time to write. Of course, it doesn't help that I'm not really a great writer."

"Is Ms. Perrelli here with you then?"

"No, not this time. Actually, I just needed a few days away, and Outlandish seemed the perfect place to run away to. I really love it here."

Annella played with the tops of her scallions. "Shall I tell Archie you're here? I'm going straight home after I check out."

Tallie blushed. "Oh, well, I guess you could tell him I'm here. I mean, I don't want to bother him if he's busy."

Annella rolled her eyes and chuckled. "I'm certain he isn't too busy to see you."

Tallie looked relieved.

"I'm working tonight and Albert is out of town, so Archie will be eating at the restaurant. Why don't you surprise him?"

Tallie looked a little uncertain. "Do you think I should?"

"I do," Annella said with a playful expression.

"Well, okay," Tallie answered. "That does sound kind of fun. I'm just grabbing a few things for my stay. I'll pop by the restaurant later. What time do you think he'll be there?"

"He's usually there by six."

Annella grabbed Tallie's hand and squeezed it. "He'll be so happy to see you, dear."

Tallie waited until six-fifteen just to be sure Archie would already be there. She hadn't felt so nervous in a long time. When she walked in, she saw a band setting up by the dance floor, she also saw Archie at his table with his head down and a book open in front of him. Her heart began to race at the sight of him. She stood for a moment trying to decide how to approach him. Would she say something clever or just walk over and say "Hi"? While she was trying to decide, the hostess said, "One for dinner tonight?"

"Oh, no," Tallie said. "Um, I'm here to see Archibald."

The lady pointed to him. "He's at his table."

"Yes, I see that," said Tallie. "I'll just go on over. Thank you."

The hostess smiled and turned back to her guest book.

Tallie was out of time for coming up with anything clever to say, so she just cleared her mind and decided she'd say whatever came out in the moment . . . which ended up being, "Is this seat taken?"

Archie knew her voice immediately and turned to see her. "Tallie!"

It wasn't like Archie to show excitement quite like he did in that moment, but he was so surprised to see Tallie that it happened before he could stop it. He stood up and rather than taking time to open his umbrella to go to her, he put his hand out to her. When she took his hand, he pulled her into a hug.

Stepping back, she smiled and said, "I was so nervous about just popping in on you like this, but your mother suggested I surprise you."

"My mother?"

"Yes, I ran into her at the market today."

"Did she know you were coming?"

"No, no. I really did just run into her. She was as surprised as you are. I was going to write to you first, but I didn't want to have to wait for your response. I was just so ready to get away . . . like yesterday."

Archie motioned for Tallie to sit down. "Why did you need to get away? Is everything all right?"

"Oh yeah. Everything's fine. Gemma can just get a little controlling, you know? I mean, I'm thankful for her help. Don't get me wrong."

"On a first name basis now?"

Tallie didn't understand. "What do you mean?" she asked.

"Well, I've never heard you call her Gemma. It's always been Gemma Perrelli or Ms. Perrelli. And she was stubborn with me about it as well."

Archie wasn't offended, but he was bewildered by her confession and was still trying to solve the puzzle in his head.

"Well, shall we have dinner?"

Tallie examined him, trying to decide if he was upset or not. She couldn't tell, so she asked. "You're not upset with me?"

"I don't believe so," he said, putting his chin between his thumb and forefinger.

Tallie found his response to her confession terribly funny. She smiled and tried to hold back the laughter, but it didn't work. Before she knew it she *was* laughing.

Archie laughed, too, but only because Tallie was laughing.

Tallie forced herself to stop and said as seriously as she could, "I would love to . . . have dinner with you, that is."

While they were looking through the menu, the band began to play. Tallie found herself moving to the music and said, "I'm loving this music! What is it?"

"It sounds like a sort of bossa nova."

"What's a bossa nova?" asked Tallie.

"Hm. Well, technically speaking, it's Brazilian jazz . . ."

"How would you even know that?" she asked.

"Well, I'm not certain, but I think it is. This might be a variation of it, but it does sound similar."

"Are you a musician or do you just happen to know everything?"

"Mostly I just like to learn, and that must be one of the things I learned. And yes, I do play piano and play at a few other instruments."

"A few other? Sheesh." Pointing at the band, she said, "Can you play one of those? That is one massive cello!"

It was Archie's turn to suppress a laugh. "It's actually called a bass."

"Really? What's the difference?"

"I'm sure there are many differences between the two that I couldn't explain, but at a glance, the bass is much larger. Also, cellos are played while sitting down and placing the instrument between the legs, and a bass is played while standing. That's the standard method."

Tallie giggled. "As you can tell, I've never known much about music, although I did learn to play the recorder in the fifth grade."

Archie raised his eyebrows. "Well, I'd say that makes you know more than at least some."

"I suppose," Tallie said, shrugging. She then

surprised Archie by saying, "I do know a little about dancing, and this is some pretty great dancing music. You'll dance with me, won't you?"

"Noooo . . . but thank you," Archie answered. "As delighted as I am to see you, I just—"

Tallie interrupted. "Hey, I thought you said you could dance."

"I can, and I'm quite good, too, but if you remember, I said I danced in my living room . . . with my mother."

"You've never danced here at the restaurant?" Tallie asked.

Archie shook his head.

She prepared her next question in hopes of appealing to his competitive side. "Well, I'll admit, I was surprised when you said you could dance. It just didn't seem like something you would enjoy."

Archie shook his head. "I *know* what you're doing."

"That didn't make you want to change your mind?"

"Not in the least."

"Come on, don't you feel at least a little persuaded to show me your dancing skills?"

Archie shook his head and made it clear he wasn't even considering it.

"I don't believe you really can. I think you should prove it to me."

Archie only looked at her in disbelief.

"Is it your umbrella? Nobody's on the floor. We wouldn't bother anyone."

"No, Tallie, it's not my umbrella. It's my nerves. I'm simply too—"

"Afraaaaid?" Tallie asked.

"I guess I'm a little afraid."

Tallie finally surrendered. "Oh, I missed you, Archibald Plumby."

Archie changed the subject. "I really appreciate that you are willing to call me Archibald. I wonder why people are so uncomfortable with it. I *always* introduce myself as Archibald but inevitably I become Archie."

"It's weird," said Tallie. "I wonder why?"

"I've never been able to figure it out. Is it very hard to say?"

Tallie said it carefully, "Arch-ibald. Ar-chi-bald. No. It's actually really easy to say."

Archie laughed. "Maybe it's just a little too formal sounding for most people."

"What is your middle name?" Tallie asked him.

"Benjiro."

"Benjiro? I've never heard that before. What does it mean?"

"Peaceful."

"Oh, that fits you perfectly! What about the name Archibald?"

"Bold and truthful," he said, lifting his chin and showing a look of mock pride.

"Wow. Your parents did good," said Tallie.

"Well, I think so," he said with a chuckle.

"What about your name?" he asked.

"Oh, are you ready for this?" asked Tallie.

"Absolutely."

"Well. Tallie's short for, Tallulah. I'll bet you've never heard that one."

Archie replied fondly, "No, I haven't, but it's a beautiful name. Have you ever learned its meaning?"

"I'm not sure," she answered. "I think I remember my mom telling me it means 'leaping water' or something like that," she said with a laugh. "My mom's adoptive family was Native American. Tallulah was my mom's only sister who died when they were kids. She said they were super close. Anyway, almost everyone pronounced my name wrong, so I decided to start going by Tallie when I was pretty young."

"That makes sense. And Tallie suits you. What about your middle name?"

"I don't have a middle name. I mean, I do, but it's only a letter."

"A letter?" questioned Archie.

"I know, that's weird, isn't it? My mom was a little eccentric."

"I don't think it's weird. But which letter?"

"Z," Tallie answered. "Tallulah Z. Greenleaf."

"So, Tallulah Z., shall we order our dinner?"

"Well, Mr. Archibald Benjiro, what do you recommend?"

"I recommend it all. My mother *is* the chef, after all, and I can promise you, everything is delicious. Why don't you look through the menu and see what sounds good to you?"

"Okay," she said, taking the menu from Archie.

Archie subtly admired Tallie while her attention was on the menu. He still couldn't believe she had come. When she looked up from the menu he quickly turned his head to make it appear he was looking at something else. She could tell he had been watching her, and so he wouldn't feel awkward she said quickly, "I've never liked fish much, but I've been told it's because I've never had *good* fish. So if I were going to try some, what would you recommend?"

"Have you ever eaten shrimp?" he asked.

"Only fried. I don't dislike it as much as most fish."

"Grilled shrimp is delicious and pretty mild. You could try that. Or you could try the fish tacos. Mother uses haddock, which is also a pleasant flavor. She serves the tacos with cabbage, lime, avocado, and cilantro. They're one of my favorites."

"I'll have that!" said Tallie.

Archie raised his hand to the waiter. When he walked up he said, "Hey Arch, my man. What's up?"

"Hey, Taft, we're ready to order if you're ready."

Taft pulled a pen from behind his ear and moved his long blond hair away from his eyes. "At your service, dude!"

Archie was used to Taft's laid-back manner, but Tallie was caught off guard and laughed a little. Taft, always happy to keep the mood light, laughed back.

"We'll both have the fish tacos," Archie said.

"Excellent choice." He looked at Tallie and said, "What can I get the lady to drink?"

"Oh, water's fine. No, wait. I'll have coffee, too. It's been a long day."

"Got it. More tea, Arch, my man?" he asked.

"You know, I think I'll switch to coffee," Archie said.

"Arch is gonna down some java. All right. I'm on it, dude."

When Taft walked away, Tallie whispered, "His choice of words is hilarious."

"That's Taft," said Archie. "He's Outlandish's most prominent surf bum."

"Really?"

Archie nodded. "He surfs by day and waits tables by night, and occasionally leaves for a few days to compete. Mother is very accommodating."

"Wow, I've never known anyone who surfs."

"Yes, we both know how experienced you are with coastal living."

"Gee thanks, Arch, my man!" Tallie said trying to look like Taft.

Archie laughed at her.

"How does he afford to live in Outlandish on a waiter's salary? It's expensive here!"

"Oh, he still lives at home. He's lived here his whole life. His parents sell surfboards and surfing gear."

"That's great. Are his parents surfers, too?"

"Yes, and his two sisters, but his sisters are both married now."

Taft came back with coffee and water and said, "Freshly brewed java for the man and his lady."

Archie and Tallie both reacted to his comment by laughing it off, but when Archie looked back at

Tallie, he noticed she was wearing her signature symbol of embarrassment—splotchy neck and cheeks. "I'm sorry," he said. "I guess he just . . . assumed . . . and he's not used to seeing me here with . . . women."

"Noooo?"

Archie rolled his eyes. When he looked away, he was surprised to see Luke walk into the restaurant. When Luke looked his direction, Archie waved him over.

Tallie turned to see whom he was waving at.

When Luke got to the table, Archie put his hand out and said, "Luke!"

"Hey, Arch!"

Archie looked at Tallie and said, "Tallie, this is my friend, Luke Pindabrook. Luke, Tallie Greenleaf."

Tallie shook Luke's hand. "You're the magician, right?"

Luke smiled. "One of the sixteen Pindabrooks!"

"Sixteen! Wow! I'm dying to see your show." Looking at Archie, she said, "You're going to take me to their show, right?"

"Of course."

Archie said to Luke, "Do you want to join us for dinner?"

Luke had come to the restaurant hoping to spend some time with Archie, but since Tallie was there, he didn't want to intrude, so instead he said with a smile, "No, no. I don't want to interrupt you. I just came to grab some takeout."

Tallie saw Luke wink at Archie but pretended she didn't.

"It was nice meeting you, Tallie. I hope you *will* come and see our show. I could pull you in as a volunteer if you'd like."

"That's okay," she said. "Stages freak me out."

"I've heard that one before," Luke said looking at Archie.

Tallie smiled. "I really enjoyed meeting you. Archie speaks very highly of you."

"Well, he'd better," said Luke.

Archie laughed.

"You two enjoy yourselves," he said before walking away.

"You've been friends a long time, haven't you?" asked Tallie.

"Yes, pretty much our entire lives."

"That's so great. He seems like a really nice guy."

"He is a great guy ... and currently a heartbroken one. His fiancée just broke off their engagement."

"Aw, that's so sad. How long were they together?"

Archie thought about it for a moment. "A year? Maybe a little longer. They were engaged for a couple of months."

"I hate hearing that. He's so cute though. He'll find someone else."

Archie was surprised at Tallie's words and to his shame, he felt a little jealous. He'd always known the girls thought Luke was good-looking, but it had never bothered him until that very moment. He forced himself not to linger on his jealousy and changed the subject. "How long are you staying?"

"I have a reservation for a week."

"The Lupine?" asked Archie.

"No," she said pouting. "Sadly, they were booked. In fact, every hotel was booked."

"Well, it is summer and this is a tourist town. Where are you staying?"

"I rented a little room above the Salt Boutique. It was all that was available. It's fine. I don't plan on spending much time inside. I'm hoping to see more of Outlandish this trip."

"I'll be happy to show you around," Archie said.

"Would you? I was hoping you'd say that. I know you have to work. I don't want to get in the way."

"I think I can fit you into my schedule," Archie teased. "You can come to work with me. As long as you don't distract me too much."

Tallie smacked his arm playfully. "Distract you from what . . . observing?" asked Tallie.

"Yes, and believe me, it can be done."

"Well, I can't write, but maybe I can help you observe. You can gaze one direction, and I'll gaze the other."

"Sounds perfect," said Archie.

"Speaking of observing," Tallie said. "I met the salt shop owners today. They are so interesting and their shop is incredible."

"Did you ask them about their names?" Archie asked.

"No, but I am curious. Tell me."

"Well, their parents met when they played in the Los Angeles Philharmonic. Their father played the clarinet and their mother played the piccolo, so they named their two children after their instruments."

"It sounds like their parents are as eccentric as they are," Tallie said.

"I've met them," Archie said. "They're actually pretty normal."

"What—no dreads and bare feet?"

"No, but they did get that red hair from their

parents. They're both quite redheaded," Archie said.

"So the salt shop didn't belong to their parents first?"

"No. They just moved here a few years ago and set up shop."

Tallie admitted, "I bought a couple of things from them today."

"What did you buy?"

"Well, they told me they were famous for their chocolate mint sucking salt, so I had to try it out."

"And?"

"And . . . I actually haven't tried it yet," she said laughing. "I was so nervous about coming to meet you, it hasn't even made its way out of the bag."

"Why were you nervous?"

"I wasn't sure you'd be happy about my coming unannounced."

"Are you kidding? I am delighted to see you."

"Same here," she answered, feeling herself blush. "So, what have you been up to, Archibald?"

Archie thought about what he'd been doing the past few months and realized how hard it would be to answer her question. He would either keep it light and not *really* tell Tallie what he'd been up to, or he'd be honest and that might be too hard to explain. When he hesitated, she asked, "What?"

There wasn't enough time to make a decision, so he changed the subject. "Have you heard about the sea lion pups that washed up on the beach, sick and stranded?"

"No, you can't do that. You didn't answer me," she said.

Archie looked at Tallie. "Aren't you curious about the poor sea lions though?"

"Actually, I am. But first you have to answer my question."

"The truth is, Tallie, the answer is just too complex."

"Try me," she said.

Archie sighed. "I haven't really done anything worth mentioning. It's what I've been thinking about. That's where the real story is."

"So tell me what you've been thinking about."

"How about you ask me about it after we've had some lighter conversation?"

"Fair enough."

"Now it's my turn," he said. "What have you been up to?"

"Well. I'm pretty much in the same boat. So it sounds like we should wait for that conversation until at least tomorrow."

Chapter 12

Excited about the day ahead, Archie woke about an hour earlier than usual. Realizing God had answered many prayers for him, including bringing Tallie back to Outlandish, he felt compelled to stop and thank God. Rolling out of bed, Archie sat on his floor, crossed his legs, and bowed his head.

"Lord, I feel so grateful. You've taken my life from a state of confusion and brought some clarity to it. You've given me clear direction in the way of my calling, and You've given me hope for something I wasn't sure was your will. I'll admit, when I asked You to bring Tallie back to me, I doubted it would happen. It's not that I don't find You kind and giving. You are certainly both of those things. I only doubted my reasoning in asking You for it.

"Bringing Tallie back to Outlandish was a wonderful way of reminding me You are hearing my prayers and considering my desires. I now pray I might have the courage to trust You as You lead me down a very unfamiliar path."

Archie ended his prayer with, "Thank You for my faithful, accommodating parents as well as my new and longtime friends. Thank You for allowing me to live in such a beautiful place, and for giving me a week with Tallie. Amen."

Feeling especially energetic, and because his father was out of town, Archie decided to surprise his mother by making them both an omelet. Although his culinary skills were nothing close to his mother's, he knew she would appreciate his effort, and he wanted an opportunity to spend some time with his mother.

When his father was out of town, his mother tended to sleep a little late, and Archie was happy for the extra time to prepare breakfast. Since he needed both hands to cook and needed to be able to move around the kitchen freely, Archie would need to wear his hat umbrella, which wasn't his favorite thing in the world. It was a medium sized umbrella that sat right on top of his head and was held on with an adjustable band. The canopy of the umbrella was designed to be flexible so it wouldn't pop off of his head when he accidentally nudged it with a cabinet door. He only ever let his parents see him in this contraption. He knew it made him look ridiculous, but sometimes he simply couldn't avoid it.

He went about choosing ingredients for what he considered a deluxe omelet, although he knew he'd never be able to pick just the right combination of ingredients to match his mother's perfect palate. He finally decided on eggs, clarified butter, Fontina and Gruyere cheeses, and a large portabella mushroom cap. To add flavor and to impress his mother, he would add fresh chervil, tarragon, and parsley.

He moved over to the counter where he cracked, mixed, shredded, and chopped; sautéed mushrooms; cooked eggs; and eventually assembled the first of the two omelets.

Just as he was about to remove the omelet from the pan, his mother stepped into the kitchen. Still standing a ways from Archie, she lifted her nose and inhaled. "I must have smelled that in my sleep, Archie. I was dreaming Anne Willan was in my kitchen making me breakfast."

"Who is Anne Willan?" asked Archie.

"Who is Anne Willan? Archie! You can't be serious. I've talked about her your entire life."

Archie looked at his mother blankly.

"She's a legendary chef of French Cuisine!"

"Oh yes! Anne Willan."

Annella couldn't tell if he really did remember or was just pretending, but she let him off the hook.

Archie added, "Well, I'm *no* Anne Willan, but I am making you breakfast."

Annella walked over to Archie and attempted to kiss him on the cheek but gave up. "Oh, that hat!"

"I couldn't think of a way around it."

"Well, it smells delicious," she said while inhaling deeply.

"Don't get your hopes up."

"Oh, but I am," she said. "Did you already have your breakfast?"

"Actually," he answered, "I'm going to be eating an omelet with you."

"*Really?* You're going to eat an omelet? Not your usual toast and prunes?"

"Yes, well, I thought I'd give it a whirl."

"Lovely," she said.

When his mother sat down and he put the plate in front of her, as well as a pot of tea, she took a moment to put her nose to the omelet. It was a common occurrence. She ate nothing without doing this first. She said it was "savoring it before tasting it" and it was "absolutely necessary for a chef."

"Would you be offended if I chopped up some chives to throw on top?" she asked.

Archie threw his hands up in the air and said, "Of course. Chives! That's what you always add with those three herbs. I couldn't remember!"

"Oh, well, it's almost perfect. I can tell by the aroma."

"Stay there," he said. "I'll chop the chives."

Archie hurried up about it so his mother would taste the omelet before it cooled. He took the cutting board over to his mother and sprinkled them on top.

"There. Now give it a try."

Annella put her nose to it all over again and said, "Perfect." She then cut a piece of the omelet off with her fork and took her first bite.

If Annella was dramatic about anything, it was food. She closed her eyes as she chewed, and once she had swallowed the bite said, "That's really quite delectable, Archie."

Archie smiled. Then he went back to the kitchen to cook his own omelet.

Once Archie and his mother were at the table eating together, she asked him, "So what are we celebrating this morning?"

Archie finished chewing his bite. "I wasn't exactly thinking of it as a celebration, but I suppose it might be."

"About what?"

"Well, about life in general. You encouraged me. Father counseled me. God has heard my prayers, and Tallie has come for a week. Those are enough reasons to celebrate."

Annella smiled. "Yes. Those are very good reasons to celebrate. Will you be spending the day with Tallie?"

"Yes. I think I'll be spending most of the week with her. She told me she would like to see *all* of Outlandish."

"Well, with a whole week, that shouldn't be too difficult. What are your plans?"

"I haven't come up with any just yet. Tallie is

pretty good at letting me know what she wants to do, so I think I'll just make some suggestions and let her tell me."

"Well then, there's your plan!"

Archie and Tallie met in front of the Salt Boutique at ten o'clock.

"Good morning, Mr. Plumby," she said cheerfully.

"Good morning to you, Miss Greenleaf."

"So what are we doing today?" she asked.

"Well, what do you want to start with? Something spectacular? Something charming? Or something delicious?"

Tallie put her finger on her lip and pondered. "I just had a Pop-Tart, so maybe . . ."

Before she could finish, Archie said, "Wait. You ate a Pop-Tart for breakfast?"

"Well, I'm not staying at a real hotel you know, so they don't serve breakfast. I just bought some easy breakfast food that doesn't require refrigeration or cooking."

Archie shook his head. "Not acceptable."

Tallie walked with Archie. "Where are you taking me, Archibald?"

"Be patient now," he said.

When they had walked a block and stood in front of The Lupine, he said, "Would you mind waiting out here for a few minutes?"

"Why? What're you doing?"

"Just let me check on something. I'll be right back."

It had only been a few minutes when Archie walked back out the door. "How long will it take you to pack up your stuff?"

"What? Why?"

"If we walk back to your room, how long will it take you to pack your things?" he asked again.

"Um, only a few minutes, I guess. Why?"

"Because you're staying at your favorite inn."

"I am?"

"Yes, you are."

"How? They said they were booked."

"Well, they weren't . . . at least not technically. They always have two rooms reserved for Outlandish business use. I'm qualified to reserve a room on behalf of the newspaper, though I've never done it before."

Tallie said, "But I'm not here on business. Will I have to fake it? Because I'm not very good at faking."

"No," said Archie. "I would never ask you to do that. I just told them you were a photographer here to take some pictures of Outlandish for *potential* use. It was good enough for them."

"See, you said I was here on business! I can't, Archibald! It feels wrong."

"Miss Greenleaf, are you going to be taking pictures?"

"Yeah, I'll take pictures," Tallie answered.

"And is it at least slightly possible you might use one at some point for the promotion or publicity of something or someone in Outlandish?"

"Well . . . it's possible, I guess," she said.

"Then I was completely honest, and you are perfectly entitled to the room, and if it makes you feel any better, it wouldn't have been used by anyone else this week anyway."

"I will pay though."

"You can't," said Archie. "It's a complimentary room. Several businesses in Outlandish offer services in exchange for the rooms. *Stay Afloat* is one of them. We give them free advertising in the paper. So you can't pay. It's not even an option."

"But what if—"

"Tallie," said Archie, "let's go get your things."

Of course Tallie was pleased to be staying in The Lupine Inn, but more than that, she was grateful to Archie for caring for her enough to work it out. After she took her bags up to the room and came back out to meet Archie, she hugged him and said, "You're the best, you know."

Archie scratched his cheek, looked squarely at Tallie, and said, "It seemed wrong for you to be staying anywhere but here. And Pop-Tarts! Ew!"

Tallie laughed. "Now remember, I've never lived with a chef, and I eat macaroni-and-cheese donuts for dinner!"

Archie rolled his eyes. "I can't imagine."

"Don't you ever eat junk?"

"Yes. Sometimes. Well, no, not really," he admitted.

"You should eat some junk with me while I'm here. It'll be an experience!"

"I *have* always wanted to try funnel cake," Archie admitted.

"Believe it or not, I've never had one, either," said Tallie. "I mean, not many towns have street carts with funnel cakes year-round. I've only seen them at fairs and such, but I've never actually bought one."

"Well, let's just get that out of the way right now," said Archie.

Tallie laughed. "Pop-Tarts and funnel cakes all before lunch. Are you ready to experience that version of Tallie?"

"I believe so," said Archie.

"Well, okay then."

The funnel cake cart was very near The Lupine, and it was just opening its window when they walked up.

"Good morning!" said the man behind the window. "What can I get for you?"

Tallie and Archie were staring at the menu on the side of the cart and looking a little overwhelmed when the man said, "Have you ever had a funnel cake?"

At the same time they both said, "No."

"Well, you are in for a treat, my friends. You can order a plain funnel cake which comes with only powdered sugar, or you can order it with toppings." He pointed to the toppings list and said, "And of course whipped cream is a must if you order toppings."

Tallie looked at Archie. "Let's go all out."

"All right," he answered. "You pick the toppings. Whatever you'd like."

"Oh, so much pressure. Hmmm. Let's see. How about, bananas . . . strawberries . . . chocolate syrup and whipped cream?"

"Sure," said Archie.

"Good choices, Miss. Coming right up!"

When the enormous funnel cake was prepared and Archie had paid for it, Tallie carried it to a nearby bench to eat it. Archie set up his umbrella stand and said, "I feel like we should pray and ask God to protect us from whatever this has the potential of doing to us."

"Oh come on," said Tallie. "It's just a funnel cake! And besides, it has fruit!"

"And that makes it so much better for us," said Archie sarcastically.

"It was you who suggested it. Now stop making me feel guilty."

"All right," Archie said.

She held up the plate. "You have to go first."

Archie started to refuse, but Tallie put her finger up and said, "No, no, no."

She handed the plate to Archie and he began to pinch off a little piece, but Tallie said, "Take a bigger bite than that! Oh, but wait, I want a picture!"

"Ohhhh no," he said.

"Archibald, I'm here to see Outlandish and have some fun. Let me take home some memories. Please?" she begged.

Archie smiled a crooked smile and sighed. "All right. Have it your way."

He looked around to make sure no one was looking and then pinched off a large piece of the funnel cake. Tallie stood back with her camera and waited until he put the piece to his mouth. Just as it touched his lips, a piece of banana fell on his lap. He ignored it while he shoved the funnel cake into his mouth. He turned his head away from Tallie while he chewed, but he could hear her giggling as well as taking pictures. Finally, when he was done chewing, he went to clean up his mouth, and it was then he realized they'd forgotten napkins. He tried to use his hands, but Tallie said, "Wait, let me help." She let her camera hang from a strap against her chest, pulled a napkin out of her purse, and began cleaning up the funnel cake leftovers around Archie's mouth.

"There," she said. "So what did you think? Delicious?"

"Quite, I'm afraid."

"Don't worry, I won't tell your mother."

"Thank you," said Archie. "She really would frown at such a messy presentation of ingredients."

"I'm sure she would," said Tallie.

"Now, Madame Photographer, it's your turn."

"Here," she said removing the camera from around her neck. "You can take pictures of me. Just so it's fair."

"I'm not sure I'll do it very well," he said taking the camera reluctantly.

Tallie put the strap over his head and said, "I put it on automatic for you. All you have to do is look through here and click this button." Moving away from Archie, she added, "I'll even stand back here so you can stay right under your umbrella."

"For the sake of your memories, I'll give it a whirl," he said.

Tallie tore off a piece of the cake and said, "I'm excited," before putting it in her mouth.

Archie snapped a picture of Tallie while she posed with the plate in front of her. He took another picture when she pinched off a piece and put it in her mouth.

"My piece was bigger," he said. Which made Tallie take a much larger piece and put it in her mouth.

He took another picture, then stopped to watch Tallie for a moment while she chewed. He couldn't help but laugh at the chocolate drizzle that was now on the tip of her nose.

"Don't laugh!" she said with her mouth still full.

"I'm not laughing," he said, suddenly looking very serious.

"So messy!" she mumbled through a full mouth.

Archie laughed. "But worth it, right?"

Tallie nodded, finished chewing, and reached for a third bite. "Totally!"

Chapter 13

Archie and Tallie finished their funnel cake and were tempted to go for another but resisted and went to the beach instead.

While they walked together, Tallie asked Archie, "Have we had enough light conversation to warrant a more serious one now?"

Archie acted as though he didn't know what she was referring to, but he knew exactly what she wanted to know. "Does it have to be terribly serious?"

"No," she answered shaking her head. "That's not what I meant. I'm just . . . well, I'm still wondering why you couldn't answer me when I asked what you'd been up to."

Archie nodded. "I see."

Tallie stopped walking, which made Archie stop, too. She turned to face him. "If you don't want to talk about it, it's okay. I just thought, maybe, you might want to, you know, tell me what you've been thinking about."

The day had been so pleasant that Archie hated the idea of possibly ruining it, so he decided to reveal only a little piece of what had been on his mind. "Before you left last time you encouraged me to do something. Do you remember what it was?"

"Yeah," Tallie said quickly, "I told you to keep writing."

"Children's stories," Archie said. "You told me to keep writing children's stories."

Tallie acknowledged his words with a smile and nodded.

"Your encouragement was well-timed. I had been wondering what direction my life might go in the way of a profession. Writing had been the only thing I'd ever pursued beyond hobby, but that has only been part-time work, nothing to support myself with. It's been weighing on my mind."

Tallie was quiet while he searched for the right words to continue.

"I prayed about it and eventually went to Father and asked for advice. Among other things, he encouraged me to keep my eyes and heart open. He said there was more for me out there and to search around every corner for God's will for my life. So I searched. I read everything. I talked to everyone. I went everywhere."

"I had no idea you had all of that on your mind. Have you worked anything out?" she asked.

"Yes. It was when I was in the library one day that, I believe, God revealed something valuable to me. Something that would steer me in a particular direction."

"What was it?"

"I went into the library that day to read my papers, and when I walked in, Mrs. Pinkers, the librarian, brought a book over to me. This wasn't unusual at all. Mrs. Pinkers and I have enjoyed and discussed children's books for years."

Tallie's jaw dropped open. "Oh my gosh, that's so sweet."

Archie blushed a little. "Well, she left the book with me and asked me to let her know what I thought of it. I said I would and she walked away. Only a moment later, a little girl walked up to me and asked me about my umbrella. Her name was Felicity. I had never seen her before, although it turns out she was Mrs. Pinkers' great-granddaughter. Anyway, we had a little conversation, and then she asked me to read the book to her. I wasn't at all comfortable with it, but I remembered my father's advice about keeping my eyes and heart open, so I decided I would read the book to Felicity."

Tallie grew fonder of Archie with each word he spoke.

"By the time I was finished," Archie continued, "Felicity seemed changed. I could tell the story had spoken to her. Its message seemed to leave an impact."

Archie's expression was serious when he looked at Tallie. "Tallie, a child's world is an important one. Children need stories. They need to be inspired. They need to see kindness and catch a glimpse of different lives . . . different worlds."

"I totally agree," said Tallie.

"Stories can transform people," Archie said. "I want to be a part of that. I think God wants me to be a part of that."

Tallie felt a lump in her throat so she didn't try to talk. Archie questioned her with his eyes and she waved her hands in front of her face.

"What is it?" he asked. "Are you all right?"

She finally managed to say, "I can't believe how sweet that is. I'm totally choked up."

"So now you know why I didn't want to bring it up before."

Tallie nodded. "God is definitely doing something in your life. I can't wait to see what it is."

"Now if I could only figure out what story I'm supposed to write. I've labored over it and so far every idea has been worthless."

"It'll come," Tallie said. "Just be patient and wait for it."

Archie nodded. "Are you thirsty?" he asked.

"Yeah. I am."

"What I wouldn't give for some frozen grapes."

"Frozen grapes?" Tallie asked.

"Oh. Father used to sell them from a cart before he married Mother. I've never actually had one, but they sure sound good, don't they?"

"Anything frozen . . . or even cold sounds really good right now," Tallie answered. "I'm actually really thirsty."

Archie pointed out a lemonade cart. "Will lemonade be okay?"

Tallie nodded enthusiastically.

The line was a little long, but they eventually purchased their lemonades and decided to go back into town so Tallie could take her photos of the fountain.

When they were moving toward Central Circle, Tallie's attention was drawn to a small child, a blond boy, who was leaning over the edge of the fountain.

"Oh gosh, I hope he doesn't fall in."

When Archie saw the boy, he knew immediately what he was doing, which was reaching for a coin in the fountain. Although he'd never done it himself, he'd always wanted to and had been watching children reach for coins for as long as he could remember.

The fountain wasn't deep, and the child wasn't likely to drown if he fell in, but if he were to fall head first, he might get a decent bump on his head.

The boy's determination to get to the coin made his reach quite dramatic. He was balancing on his midriff. His legs were in the air. Tallie was nervous about him being hurt, so Archie rushed over just in case.

Archie sat on the wall of the fountain next to the boy, but decided not to bother him unless he began to tumble. Tallie came and sat next to Archie and whispered, "Who do you think he belongs to?"

"I don't know," Archie answered. "Do you see any likely candidates?"

They both scanned the area but nobody stood out. Archie turned to watch the boy and saw his little fingers coming very close to seizing a penny. Realizing the boy was only moments from falling in, but also very close to getting his penny, Archie decided it was time to step in and help him. Leaning his head down a little he said, "Hey there. I'll tell you what. I'll keep you steady so you can grab it."

The little boy's eyes remained focused on the coin, so he didn't look at Archie but he did manage an "Okay."

Of course Archie only had one hand available, but his hand was large enough to wrap his fingers around the boy's ankles, so that's what he did while the little boy secured the coin in his short fingers.

When the boy pushed his body back over the edge of the fountain's rim, Archie let go of his ankles and said, "Good job."

The boy looked at Archie with large blue eyes and said, "Thank you, Mister!"

"It was my pleasure," Archie said, feeling good about helping him.

The little boy was admiring his coin when his mother finally entered the scene. "There you are, Oscar! Did you take that coin from the fountain?" she scolded.

The little boy looked up at his mother and nodded.

"Now give me that," the woman said to her son.

The boy pulled the coin closer and said, "But . . ."

His mother opened his clenched hand, took the coin from him, and threw it back into the water. "You can't steal coins from public fountains. It's against the law. Well . . . at least, I think it is."

She looked at Archie as if she expected him to tell her whether it was or not. Having no idea himself, he just shrugged.

The boy began to cry, which was no surprise to Archie. He'd witnessed his diligent effort in getting the coin and knew it must have felt like it was all for nothing. Archie looked over at the boy sympathetically and watched as his mother steered him away from the fountain. Archie still felt sorry for him. When the little boy looked back, Archie waved and so did Tallie.

A title, *Children, Please, Take a Penny from Our Fountain*, came to Archie even before he realized his mind had pegged the incident as article worthy. He usually wasn't one of the participants of his observations, and he didn't plan to let anyone know it was he who helped the little boy take the penny from the fountain, but Archie decided he would write the story, because he wanted the children who came to Outlandish to be able to do what they were forbidden to do in probably every other public fountain, which was to take a coin.

"Arrrrrchibaaaaaald."

Archie turned toward Tallie in a sort of daze and said, "Yes?"

"Where were you?" she asked.

"What do you mean?"

"I was trying to get your attention. You were totally zoned out."

"I'm sorry. Titles. Story ideas. They pop into my head without even trying. And I guess now I can be sure that they pop into my head *only* when I'm not trying."

Tallie laughed and then asked Archie, "So what was it?"

Archie said, "I think I will propose that children living in or visiting Outlandish be allowed to take pennies from the fountain, at least one. Don't you think they should be allowed to? I mean, it's only a penny."

"That kid inspired you?"

"Yes. You see, for children, it isn't about the value of the money. It's the experience. What if he thought there was magic in that penny?"

It was as if he forgot he was talking to Tallie, because he handed her the umbrella, saying, "Will you hold this above me for a..." letting his words just trail off. He pulled a little notebook out of his pocket and began writing a few key points to remember.

Finally remembering where he was and whom he was with, he said, "Oh, I'm sorry," and took the umbrella from Tallie. "Would you mind if we went back to my place so I can type up this article? Or maybe you want to get settled into The Lupine, and we can meet for dinner?"

Tallie laughed. "So that's how it works, huh?"

Archie looked confused.

"Seriously, that was impressive. When an idea clicks, it really clicks, doesn't it?"

Archie finally laughed at himself. "Yes, I suppose it does just . . . click."

Tallie stood up. "Okay, well, why don't you run off and clear your mind, and I'll get my photographs of the fountain, and, hey, I might even take a nap."

"You *should* take a nap. I mean, if you would like to."

"So, *do* you want to meet for dinner?" she asked.

Archie stood. "Yes, I do. I'll pick you up at The Lupine at, let's say, seven o'clock?"

Archie's article took no time at all to write, and the final paragraph left him feeling very satisfied.

Outlandish is known for its charms and delights. People come to be entertained by exceptional performers, to eat delectable food, to buy unique merchandise, and to experience the stunning beauty of California's central coast. I propose that henceforth it will also be known as a place where imaginations are nourished and dreamers are cheered by allowing our fountain to contribute a penny a day to each child who wishes to reach in and pull one out.

When he was finished typing, he put the article in a folder labeled Articles To Be Submitted, and because he felt a little wiped out from the mental effort and still had a couple of hours before he was supposed to meet Tallie, he, too, decided to take a nap.

Archie was prone to strange dreams, but the one he had while taking his nap left him feeling troubled.

In his dream, he was standing on the beach near the water, and his feet were just beginning to get wet. He could see an enormous wave coming and knew it was going to cover him entirely, but he couldn't move away. It was as though the sand had turned to putty and his feet were firmly stuck.

He tried to yell for help, but his voice was only a whisper, and no one could hear him.

The wave was growing to an enormous size, but it was moving toward him in slow motion, and somehow it gave him a feeling of hope for being rescued. He tried his voice again, but it was still quiet. He tried to free his feet from the thick sand, but they were still stuck. His heart began to race, and he looked down and watched his chest move to the rhythm of his heartbeat.

He looked up and saw Tallie on the stairs of the beach waving to him. She was laughing, but he could tell it wasn't at his predicament. It was as if she didn't realize what was about to hit him, and she seemed to be happy about leaving him there. He tried to yell to her, but his voice barely reached his own ears.

"Tallie! Don't leave! I neeeeed yoooou!" was his whispered cry.

The fear subsided for a moment as the grief of Tallie leaving penetrated his heart. It was broken in a way it had never been broken before. His chest felt heavy. He pressed his hands against it trying to relieve the pain.

The wave suddenly crashed against him and pulled him into the water. Archie's umbrella went flying, so he instinctively covered his head with his arms. His body was thrown around in the water. The panic that struck was a familiar feeling to him and because of that, he told himself to breathe through it, but with the element of water added to the panic, he found it impossible to recover. Every time he attempted to breathe in a pattern, he was pulled back underneath the water.

With the water covering him, he tried to swim underneath it, but everything was black, and he didn't know which direction he swam. He continued to fight, making no headway, but then he heard a loud, commanding voice say, "Have courage," and without any effort at all he was instantly standing away from the water with his umbrella above him. He was dry, no longer struggling. Tallie was no longer waving, but he could still see her, and she was walking away from him. Somehow he knew she was smiling, and it hurt him.

He reached toward her with one arm, and it stretched all the way across the beach and to the stairs, but she was still beyond his reach.

Archie yelled, "Tallie!" and it was the first time his voice worked, but then he awoke, realizing he'd said it out loud. His hand was stretched out, pushing against the canopy of his bed.

He was left with a version of the panic he felt in his dream and also with a deep sadness over Tallie leaving him. He lay still, trying to recall the dream, but when he glanced the direction of the clock, he remembered his dinner with Tallie.

He hurried out of bed, quickly changed his clothes, and rushed out the door at five minutes till seven.

Archie was a little late and still working on his mood after his dream, but when he arrived at The Lupine, Tallie wasn't there. He considered going in to see if she was waiting inside, but then she came through the door in a hurry.

She was still pulling on her sweater when she said, "I'm so sorry, Archibald! I didn't realize how exhausted I was. I slept way too long!"

Archie laughed, realizing their time together must have done them both in. "That's all right. I actually just arrived myself."

"Are you as hungry as I am?" she asked.

"At least. Where would you like to go?"

"Your mother's food sounds delicious. And I'm sure it's the best anyway."

"Well, of course. She's not working tonight, but she's trained her cooks well."

"Great. I'll try other places while I'm here, I promise, but as tired as I still am, your cozy little table back in the corner of the restaurant sounds perfect."

They didn't talk much as they walked up the short cliff to Flavors of the Earth, and after seating themselves and ordering, they seemed to be having trouble striking up a conversation.

Tallie finally asked, "Are you all right?"

Archie perked up as much as he could. "Yes. I'm fine."

"You just seem a little unlike yourself tonight."

"I am a little out of sorts, but I'm sure I'll snap out of it."

"Are you sure? Did something happen?"

Archie hesitated and Tallie persisted. "If you need to talk . . . ?"

Archie sighed. "Your mention of a nap earlier must have predisposed me to one, because when I was finished writing my article, I went to sleep. I slept much too long and had to rush to meet you. I don't think I've quite perked up. That's all."

Tallie laughed. "How funny. We must have worn each other out today!"

"Though I'm not sure why," Archie said with a chuckle. "All we did was eat and walk."

"We walked for a long time," said Tallie. "But you forgot to mention all the talking. Talking that much is exhausting."

Taft, who was waiting tables that night, brought Archie and Tallie their salads and topped them with freshly ground black pepper. Before walking away he said, "The rest will be out soon, dudes. Enjoy!"

Tallie laughed. "Did he just call me 'dude'?"

Archie was staring out the window and didn't respond.

Tallie looked at him seriously. "Okay. You're *not* just tired. Something *is* wrong. What is it?"

Archie raised his eyebrows and shook his head a little.

"I mean, unless it's too personal to talk about."

Archie was surprised how at ease he felt around Tallie. He felt like he'd known her forever. "It was just a dream," he said. "I'm having a little trouble shaking it off. It was so strange."

"How? What was it about?" she asked.

"I was on the beach with my umbrella, and I couldn't move from the spot I was standing in. I tried to get away when I saw a huge wave coming, but no matter how hard I tried, I couldn't move. It eventually smothered me and I lost my umbrella, which sent me into a panic, even in my dream."

"Oh, wow," Tallie interjected. "That sounds terrifying."

"It was."

"Was that it?" Tallie asked.

Archie tried to figure out how he could either avoid the question or give her an answer without it being the whole answer. He didn't want to lie, but the thought did cross his mind. He sat quietly trying to decide what to do.

"You don't have to tell me," Tallie said. "I'm not trying to pry or bring it all back. I just wanted to see if I could help."

"Thank you," he said. "May I ask you something?"

"Sure."

"Why do you work with Ms. Perrelli? Is it just to learn photography or is it something else?"

Tallie looked thoughtful but didn't answer immediately.

Suddenly feeling insecure about his question, Archie added, "Is that too nosy to ask? I don't mean to pry either."

"No," said Tallie. "I'm just trying to come up with an honest answer. I haven't ever really thought much about it."

Archie surprised himself by asking, "Does she not drive you crazy?"

Tallie knew how Archie felt about Gemma, but she was a little surprised to hear him say it so plainly.

"No, not exactly crazy," she said. "I mean, she is a little domineering."

Archie seemed agitated. "A little? What is it like when you're working together? Does she treat you with respect and let you do things your own way, or do you feel obligated to do everything she says?"

"Well, if I'm being completely honest, she *does* actually drive me a little crazy. That's why I'm here. I really needed to get away so I could think for myself. I do think she's only trying to be helpful, well . . . mostly, but sometimes she tries to get involved in my personal life and even mocks me for some of the decisions I make. I really do want her help with photography, but . . . well, she's even trying to keep me away from . . ."

Tallie stopped, and Archie said, "From me?"

Tallie hesitated, and Archie said, "It's true, isn't it?"

She nodded, and Archie asked, "Does she tell you why?"

"No," said Tallie. "That's what I don't understand. When I ask her why, she won't give me an answer. She just keeps telling me I need to stay focused and if I really want to be a photographer, I need to find success before I . . . well, you know."

"Do you agree with her?" asked Archie.

"I don't know," said Tallie. "Her success is a little intimidating. I don't want to screw things up. I guess I feel like I have to do what she recommends or she might dump me. With my mom gone, I don't want this opportunity to go away. I don't want to end up back in Kansas City working as a waitress. I can't live like that forever, Archibald."

Archie looked at Tallie sympathetically. "You're a little scared about your future, aren't you?"

Tallie felt her eyes well up so she quickly looked away.

"I'm sorry," said Archie. "Should we talk about something else?"

Tallie was trying to hold back tears when she said, "No, you're right. I am afraid. I'm afraid I'll end up alone, and that I'll have nothing. I don't have anyone, Archibald. You're so blessed to have your parents. To have Gemma take an interest in me gives me a boost of confidence and gives me hope that I might at least find a way to be by myself without needing to depend on anyone else."

Archie nodded. "That makes perfect sense."

Tallie wiped her eyes.

"You're not alone, Tallie. I do have wonderful and supportive parents, but I want the same thing as you do. I'm trying to find my own way, to have something of my own. I'm still trying to figure out what that is. I do have my family to lean on, and maybe that makes my situation a little less upsetting, but I know there is more for me and honestly, I'm on my own search to find it. I suppose we just take one day at a time and see where it leads us?"

"Yeah, I guess so."

Archie shifted in his chair. "I do want to ask you something though."

"What?" asked Tallie.

"What do you know about Gemma Perrelli's past?"

"Not much," said Tallie. "I haven't really asked her anything about it."

"You didn't know she went to college to study horticulture?"

Tallie was surprised. "No! Really? How do you know that?"

"She told me," Archie answered. "It's very interesting she told me and she hasn't mentioned it at all to you."

"Weird," said Tallie. "Why didn't she keep studying horticulture?"

"She met a guy during that time who taught her photography. She didn't say it was romantic, but I'm guessing it was. She won a prestigious competition, which led to her accidental success, and she dropped out of college to follow that success. I imagine she's advising you against getting to know me better because she's hoping to keep you from making the same mistake."

Before Tallie could respond, Taft brought their meals to the table. "Clam chowder for the lady," he said putting the bowl in front of Tallie, "and shrimp and scallops for Arch, my man."

They both thanked Taft and went back to their conversation.

"But why? She doesn't care about me. Why would my life matter to her?"

"It may not so much," said Archie. "She might be doing it for her own satisfaction. I didn't mention it before, but she wanted to do, as she put it, a little experiment with me."

"What do you mean? What kind of experiment?" asked Tallie.

"One that would hopefully cure me of my need for an umbrella. I told her I wasn't interested, but she was unrelenting. Eventually I just had to walk away."

"Weird," said Tallie.

"It is," Archie said. "I think her dissatisfaction with her own life has put her on a search for fulfillment, and since she hasn't found it personally, she might be hoping to get it another way."

"I remember you mentioning that last time I was here. Did she tell you she wasn't satisfied?"

"In a roundabout way she did. She said she'd grown up watching everyone around her reach a place of discontentment, as though they'd lost something. She admitted she'd lost it as well. She said she liked the enthusiasm of young people and that was why she was working with you."

"That kind of makes me feel sorry for her, but it kind of freaks me out a little bit, too."

"Just be careful," said Archie. "Please don't let her control your life. Make your own decisions. All right?"

Tallie nodded. "Yeah, I will."

Chapter 14

Archie intended to work while Tallie was in Outlandish, but the reality was, while Tallie was with him, he wanted nothing more than to be with her.

She only had two more days in Outlandish, and they'd done just about everything Archie could think of. They'd watched the Pindabrooks perform their spectacular magic show twice, and enjoyed coffee with Luke. They had also visited all of the shops in Outlandish so Tallie could buy a few souvenirs before she went home. They watched a musical called *Margaret and the Enchanted Lipstick* at the dinner theater, as well as ate all the best (or at least most interesting) food in Outlandish. They spent their evenings on the beach so Tallie could photograph the sunsets and even toured Outlandish on a carriage pulled behind a black, hairy-footed Shire horse.

Other than walking under Archie's umbrella together, neither Archie nor Tallie had shown any physical attention to one another, except for subtle nuances of growing affection. They were getting along marvelously, and they were also both pretty certain the other wouldn't have minded holding hands or something of that nature, but because Archie was cautious and Tallie wasn't willing to put

their friendship on the line, they both exercised impressive self-control.

Tallie had just had lunch with Archie's family out on the same porch that held his mother's herbs. They'd eaten pasta salad and lemon poppy-seed bread, and Archie's mother had just served them tea.

As they sat around the table, Tallie asked Annella, "How many different varieties of herbs do you have? I can't believe how good it smells out here."

"Oh, I don't know," she answered, "I've lost count by now. I just keep adding more and more."

"What herb do you use the most?"

"Parsley. Definitely. Although I do use more than one variety."

"I didn't know there was more than one variety. What types of food do you use it on?" asked Tallie.

"Almost everything. It goes well with fish, steak, chicken, lamb, vegetables . . ."

"I wish I could cook," admitted Tallie. "I only know how to make very basic things."

"I would love to spend some time with you in the kitchen," said Annella. "If you ever want to learn, you just let me know. I'll take you to the restaurant and let you observe for a while and when you're ready to try your hand at it, I'll give you some pointers."

"Would you? That is so sweet! My mom wasn't much of a cook and since it was just the two of us, we ate out a lot."

"I'm so sorry to hear about your mother, Tallie. It must be so hard for you. If you ever need anything, please don't hesitate to ask."

Tallie nodded with a hint of sadness in her expression. Annella reached her hand across the table and took hold of Tallie's hand with both of hers. "Those aren't empty words, Tallie. I know I could never even begin to fill that place in your heart, nor would I want to, but if I can ease the pain or be useful in any way, just know I would be happy to try."

The lump in Tallie's throat was too large to speak through, so she just smiled at Annella and let her eyes fill up with tears. It had been a while since anyone had consoled Tallie in her loss, and it felt good to be able to express her sadness over it in front of someone who seemed to sympathize and who wanted to help.

Archie was quiet but he listened to every word that passed between his mother and Tallie and was emotionally stirred by Tallie's sorrow. He didn't know what sort of response would be appropriate. He thought about saying, "I'm sorry," but wondered if it would be too conventional, especially since he'd already said it. He even contemplated joining one of his hands together with theirs, but quickly decided it would feel strange, even if it were a kind gesture. So he didn't do anything and later felt sorry for it.

That evening as Archie and Tallie sat together on the beach waiting for the sun to set, Tallie said, "Archibald, I know you struggled as a child, but were you always happy?"

"Unquestionably."

"Really? You never got bitter or angry at your circumstances?"

Archie shook his head. "I might have under different circumstances, but my parents never presented it as a viable option. Every single time I complained, they reassured me God didn't make any mistakes when He offered me life on this earth."

"So you accepted it because you felt God allowed it in your life for a reason?"

"Yes," he answered. "I was presented to my parents in a somewhat peculiar fashion and nothing could be done to change it, so my resolve was there must be some very good reason for it."

Tallie sighed. "Archibald, I want to see life like that. I try to, but I don't always do a good job of it." She turned to face him. "Your childhood was like a fairy tale and it wasn't because you had everything a child could dream of. It was because you found happiness right in the middle of your *peculiar* circumstances. I think you're pretty wonderful, Archibald Plumby."

Archie was a little embarrassed by the attention but also flattered and suspected his expression revealed it. He startled when Tallie quickly grabbed his hand excitedly and said, "Write about your childhood, Archibald! You've lived what most kids only dream of!"

He questioned Tallie with his expression.

"I don't mean you didn't struggle," she added. "That's obvious, but you were happy and so many children aren't . . . even when they've been given everything. Archibald, your physical life is so endearing with all your colorful umbrellas, and living underneath things, but it's your perspective that's so inspiring. Kids would love to read about your childhood. It would be amusing and motivating. Think of it!"

Archie seemed to be immediately struck with the same vision Tallie was presenting him. "I think I could write it, but I'm not sure I could illustrate it well," said Archie.

"I've seen your illustrations," said Tallie. "They're good. You have your own thing going on. Kids would love it."

"But my handicap is I can only draw by using a reference photo. I can't draw from my head or from real life."

"That's not a handicap. It's just your way. We could set up the scenes as you see them, or describe them in your writing, and I could photograph them. Then you would have your reference photo.

Do you have photographs of you as a child . . . and your parents?"

"I'm fairly certain we have plenty of photographs."

"Well, you could use those, too, but for the scenes you and I set up together, I'll just edit you and your parents into the photos I take. It would be easy!"

Archie looked impressed. "That might work. Yes, you could be onto something."

"I totally am! You have to do it!"

Archie nodded slowly while processing it all. Eventually he looked at Tallie and said, "Is it possible that you, Tallulah Z. Greenleaf, are providing the answer to the most profound question of my last few months?"

"Yes," she answered simply and quickly. "I am."

They both laughed at her confidence.

"Is it strange that the title for the story has already popped into my head?"

Tallie laughed, "Titles are where you begin, right?"

"Always."

"So what is it?" asked Tallie.

"*Archie Underneath?*" he said with a question in his voice.

"Oh my gosh! It's perfect!" she exclaimed. "But you prefer Archibald. Maybe you should use that."

He shook his head. "Archie is what everyone has called me, so if I'm being true to my childhood, it should be Archie."

Tallie hugged him and with her arms still around his neck said, "I'm more excited about this than I've been about anything in a long time!"

When she released him, Archie took one of her hands into his and held it for a moment. Looking into Tallie's eyes, he lifted her hand to his lips and kissed it. It wasn't something he planned, but he'd always regarded the organic expressions of love as the most cherished.

Tallie's neck began to show its usual red splotches, and so Archie said, "I'm sorry. I embarrassed you, didn't I?"

Tallie put her free hand on her neck and said with a smile, "I guess they might be induced by charm as well."

"Well, thank you for setting my mind at ease."

Not quite knowing where the conversation should go from there, Archie and Tallie sat hand in hand, focusing their eyes on the sea, but their minds were only on their hearts.

Chapter 15

Archie didn't get home until nearly eleven o'clock that night, and since he was meeting Tallie at The Lupine for breakfast at eight-thirty, he knew he should have gone to bed, but he was so eager to begin writing that he couldn't help himself. He pulled out his notebook and began formulating his story.

The title, *Archie Underneath*, kept popping into Archie's head. Would he use it as part of the story, maybe as a repeated phrase? He wasn't sure, but he would keep that in mind as he wrote. Either way, he was dead set on the title, because titles, to Archie, were practically prophetic.

Archie scribbled ideas in his notebook for four hours and by the time he decided to force himself to be finished for the night, he had already come up with a rough sketch of the story. He was excited to tell Tallie about it and hoped he would be able to pull himself out of bed in time to meet her for breakfast.

It wasn't like Archie to be late anywhere, but the excitement of the week, as well as a repeat of the nightmare he'd had a few nights before had worn him out. He rushed into The Lupine thirty minutes late and saw Tallie leaning against a wall by the inn looking through a newspaper.

He hurried over to her and said, "I'm so sorry I'm late, Tallie. I was up much too late . . . or early, depending on how you look at it."

Tallie smiled and reached out for his hand. "Don't worry about it. You were writing, weren't you?"

"How did you know?"

"Remember, I watched you rush off to write your article about the fountain incident. I saw that same look in your eyes last night. I could tell you were dying to get started."

"That is how I work. I become inspired and forget everything until I've at least put my thoughts down on paper."

"I saw they posted your article about the fountain this morning. Do you think people will like it?"

"I have no idea, but I'll know soon. People don't waste time sharing their opinion."

"Well, I read it and I think it's wonderful. It must feel great speaking on behalf of the kids in Outlandish."

"It does," he admitted.

"Well, I admire you for it."

Drinking their coffee and waiting on their breakfast, Archie said, "So today is it."

"Yeah, I guess it is."

Archie shook his head. "I've had such a wonderful time with you this week. I'm not quite sure how successful I'll be at resuming regular life."

Tallie laughed. "I was thinking the same thing. Going back to Portland sounds so dull in comparison. I mean, I like Portland, but it's missing something, you know . . ."

"What is Portland missing?" he asked completely missing the obvious meaning of her words.

Tallie looked at him expecting him to be teasing, but when he sat waiting for an answer, she felt embarrassed.

It hit him suddenly. "Oh. You mean . . . I see."

She laughed and shook her head. "Well, that was awkward."

"I'm sorry," he said chuckling. "I'm just not, well, experienced in such matters."

"And that's what's so appealing, Archibald. You're so different from everyone I've ever met. You're open and honest, but kind and gentle, too. You're just so . . . genuine."

Archie smiled. "Thanks. I don't think many see me like you do."

"Oh, I don't know," said Tallie. "I think everyone who gets to know you finds you exactly as you are. I don't think you could hide if you wanted to."

"Don't forget, that's exactly what I did when I first saw you heading toward me."

"But see, even that was a genuine reflection of who you are. There are so many things you could have done, even feeling as insecure as you obviously did. But you did what you were inclined to do instead, and I admire that."

Archie remained quiet but seemed pleased with Tallie's observations.

"Have you ever had a . . . romantic relationship?" Tallie asked.

Archie shook his head and looked off in another direction, feeling a little conspicuous.

"Don't feel bad about it. I mean, you're only twenty, right?"

Archie nodded and again, looked away.

"Okay, no more of that. I can tell it makes you uncomfortable."

"I'm sorry," Archie said, embarrassed.

"So, tell me, what did you come up with during your sleepless night?"

"A rough draft."

"What? Of the whole story?" she asked in disbelief.

"Oh, it's a very rough draft, but I have it sketched out."

"I guess when you've got it, you've got it. I'm telling you, Archibald Plumby. This is your destiny."

She pointed to his backpack on the floor. "Did you bring it with you?"

Archie nodded. "Would you like to see it?"

"Of course!"

When Archie reached for his backpack, his elbow hit his umbrella stand, and it toppled so he lost his shelter. This did happen on occasion, and it was always a little traumatic when it did. Archie quickly ducked his head down and put his arms up over his head as if the ceiling were crashing down on him.

Tallie was caught off guard by his dramatic response and only gasped.

Archie kept his head down and asked, "Tallie, can I get a little help?" He said it calmly but he felt anything but calm.

"Oh yeah. Sorry!" she said, rushing over to him. She picked up the umbrella and stand and positioned it so it was right next to Archie. "Okay, you're all set."

When he came up, his face was pale and Tallie said, "Oh my gosh, are you okay?"

He nodded. "Just give me a moment. I'll be fine."

Tallie stood and watched Archie closely as he breathed and regained some color in his face.

"I didn't realize. I mean, it really is a big deal, isn't it?"

"Yes. A very big deal, I'm afraid."

Tallie sat next to Archie and rubbed his back, but Archie was a bit humiliated by the whole thing, and he was embarrassed by Tallie's back rub, even if she was being kind.

"Can I do anything to help?" she asked.

"Usually I recover pretty quickly if I'm left alone for a moment. It's the breathing that helps the most."

Tallie removed her hand from his back. "Oh, I'm sorry. Okay, should I leave? Or . . ."

"No, if you could just go back to your seat please, I promise I'll perk up soon."

Tallie went back to her seat. She wasn't sure if she should talk or just remain quiet, so she was pleased to hear Archie say, "If you'll grab my bag, I'll hold onto the stand this time."

"Sure."

She put the bag on the table. "Shall we try again?" he asked.

"If you're up to it."

"Of course."

Tallie was happy to see the waiter on his way to their table with their breakfast. She knew it would help them to recover from the awkward event.

They sat together for the next hour reading through Archie's ideas and talking about the reference photos she would provide for his story.

"So, maybe we should go to your house after breakfast, and I'll get pictures of your bedroom and your dining table, and we'll set up different scenes in your house and on the beach with forts and umbrellas, and you can get me some pictures of you when you were a child."

"This will be so helpful," he said. "Thank you for suggesting it."

"No problem. When I get back home, I'll edit you into the photos, print them, and send them to you. Would eight by ten be a good size to send?"

"Yes, that should work well."

"I'm so excited to see this come together! I'll get right to work on it."

"What will Gemma think about our working together?" Archie asked.

"It'll be my personal project. She won't even know about it."

"I hate to make things awkward for you. I know she keeps you pretty busy. Are you sure you want to do this for me? You can back out right now. It won't hurt my feelings.

"Besides, you've been gone all week. She's likely already a little upset about that."

"No, it'll be all right," Tallie answered. "She was working on a project I wasn't involved in, so I'm sure she didn't miss me. Should I try to get her to recommend an agent? I'll bet she knows a few. I could tell her it's for a friend. I wouldn't need to mention your name."

Archie shook his head. "I'd rather avoid that if you don't mind."

"But what if you can't find an agent on your own? I think that's pretty important with a first project, and I've heard it's really hard to get one. Let me ask her."

Archie thought about it for a moment and then said, "Let me give it a whirl and see what I come up with first. You never know, I might get lucky."

"Okay, but don't be too stubborn. It's not like you'd be selling your soul to the devil or anything."

"No?" Archie asked.

"Archibald!"

"I'm only joking," he said, chuckling.

Archie's mother was home cleaning the house when he and Tallie showed up.

"Hello, you two. What are you up to this morning?"

"Good morning, Mrs. Plumby. Has Archie told you about his book project yet?"

Archie interjected. "I ran out the door so fast this morning, I barely made eye contact with Mother and Father. In fact, I didn't."

"Well, tell her now."

Archie proceeded to tell his mother he was going to write about his childhood and that it would be in the form of a children's book.

Annella hugged Archie. "That's a wonderful idea, Archie. How did you come up with it?"

Archie put his hand out as if presenting Tallie.

"Oh Tallie, good for you! And Archie, I'm so

proud of you. What a big undertaking. One I'm sure God will bless. I always knew He had something special planned for you and your writing."

"Thank you, Mother. It's beginning to seem like the inevitable path for me. I feel it's being confirmed at every turn. Of course, we'll see whether I can truly find success in it."

"I'm going to create some reference photos for his illustrations," Tallie interjected. "That's what we came here to do this morning."

"Well, I should let you get to work then, shouldn't I?" said Annella.

"Yes, I guess we should get to work," said Tallie. "But can I get something from you, Mrs. Plumby?"

"Sure," she said. "What do you need, dear?"

"Pictures of Archibald when he was little, well, of you and Mr. Plumby as well. Do you have some you can get to easily?"

"Yes, I think I can find some," she answered. "I'll look for them while you both get started."

It took a few hours for Tallie to get all of the photos, because they needed to create each scene Archie had planned to write about, and when they finally finished, they realized they had missed lunch and were approaching the dinner hour.

"Would you like to go for some shrimp scampi?" Archie asked.

"Sure, what is it?" asked Tallie.

"Very large, succulent pieces of buttery, garlic shrimp."

Tallie laughed at Archie's dramatic description. "It does sound delicious, and I am starving."

Archie and Tallie finished their meal and decided to end their day on the beach together. Archie brought along his very large umbrella, secured it in the sand with a spike, and they both sat underneath it.

"What time do you leave tomorrow?" Archie asked.

"My flight leaves at noon, and I have to get a taxi to take me to the airport, so I'll probably leave here at about eight."

Archie smiled at Tallie. "I'm glad I'll be busy writing or I might miss you a great deal."

Tallie smiled back. "Oh, you *might*, huh?"

Archie laughed.

"Well, I know I'll miss you, Archibald."

"When do you think you'll be back to Outlandish? I hope it'll be soon."

"I hope so too, but I really don't know."

"You will write to me though?" Archie asked.

"Of course I will. And you better write back... or will you be too busy writing your book?" she teased. "I think I'll be able to squeeze it in."

Archie met Tallie at The Lupine for breakfast at seven o'clock the following morning. They talked while they ate, but kept the conversation light. It seemed neither of them wanted to think about being apart from one another. But when it was almost time for Tallie to leave, suddenly the conversation took a quick turn in the direction of parting words.

Tallie was the one to start. "Archibald, I followed you that day, months ago, only because I wanted to photograph you, but you turned out to be so much more interesting than I ever expected. I feel like I've made a wonderful friend, especially this past week. Thank you for sacrificing your schedule for me."

Archie was surprised when she used the word *friend*, and because he was cautious in his manner and inexperienced in the ways of love, he decided to refrain from saying what he thought he might, which was that he was falling in love.

Instead he said, "It was my pleasure showing you around Outlandish. I'll be happy to do it again when you come back."

"Now you create an amazing story, and I'll send you the photos as soon as I get them edited and printed. Okay?"

Archie nodded and said, "I'll do my best to impress you, Miss Greenleaf."

"I'm sure you will," she answered.

Surprised by Tallie's slight disconnect emotionally, Archie asked, "Is everything all right, Tallie?"

"Yes, why?" she asked.

"I was just . . . you seem a little . . . well, you have a long day ahead of you."

"Yes, I'll admit, I'm not a very good traveler. In fact, this was my first solo flight."

"Well, that's one more than I have."

"You've never flown?" asked Tallie.

Archie pointed up to his umbrella.

"Yes," Tallie said, "that might pose a little problem in an airplane, although wouldn't be completely impossible. I don't think."

"Why don't you let me walk you to your taxi?"

"I don't know," said Tallie.

"Why?" Archie asked. "I won't make you late."

"I know," she said. "It's just that I kinda . . ."

Archie stopped her. "Please?"

"Oh, okay," she said, although she was ready to get the good-bye over with. Her cover up emotionally was always to ignore the reality of a situation. Avoidance often worked, at least until she could be alone. In other words, Tallie hated good-byes.

What she hadn't considered, however, was how Archie would perceive her manner, and it was obvious he was troubled by it.

To try to set his mind at ease, she said, "You're right, it'll be a long day, but at least my bed is waiting on the other side of it."

They walked together to the parking garage, which was only three blocks from The Lupine. Tallie carried her bag in one hand and her purse over her shoulder. Archie carried his umbrella stand's strap over one shoulder, and his umbrella in one hand. So, that meant they each had one free hand, and while they both wished to hold the hand of the other, for some reason, they didn't.

When they arrived at the parking garage, they saw Tallie's taxi was already waiting. Archie was disappointed he wouldn't have more time to say good-bye, but Tallie was relieved.

Archie helped her put her small bag in the backseat and Tallie started to climb in.

"Wait, Tallie," Archie said with a little desperation.

He took her hand and guided her back out of the taxi. She kept her head down, so Archie lifted her chin with his finger. When she looked up he saw she was crying. Her behavior made sense to him as soon as he saw her tears. "Please come back to Outlandish soon," he said. "I think . . . I mean, I can't be certain, but . . . I might be . . . well, I am actually . . ."

"What?" she asked. "You are what, Archibald?"

"I'm falling in love with you, Tallie."

What Tallie wanted to avoid, and yet deeply wished might happen, caused the reaction she feared. She began to cry, and very hard.

Archie put the back of his hand on her cheek and began wiping away her tears. Desperate for her to stop crying, he said, "Please don't cry, Tallie. I didn't mean to . . ."

With tangled feelings of joy and sadness, Tallie began laughing through her tears.

"Now you know why I was trying to leave quickly," she said.

Archie nodded. "I'm sorry."

With both hands she wiped her tears while she laughed at herself.

Archie took one of her hands and moved it away from her face. He then reached up to the other hand and took it into his. Stepping closer to Tallie, he leaned down and gently kissed her. It was something he had been nervous about beforehand, but when he kissed her, it felt natural . . . even easy. When their lips parted, they kept their faces close.

"I do love you, Tallie," Archie said quietly.

Tallie looked at Archie and smiled shyly. "I love you, Archibald."

"I'll be back. I promise," she said.

Archie kissed her hand. "I'll be here waiting."

Tallie kept his hand as she moved into the backseat of the cab. When they finally let go, Archie closed the door.

She looked out the window and waved to Archie. He smiled and watched as the cab sped away from Outlandish.

Chapter 16

Archie's article got so much positive attention that his fountain proposal was actually implemented in Outlandish after a town vote. A large sign was posted near the fountain. It read just as Archie suggested in his title: CHILDREN, PLEASE, TAKE A PENNY FROM OUR FOUNTAIN and in smaller print it said, LIMIT 1 PER DAY, PLEASE.

Archie couldn't help but be proud of his little victory. As Tallie had suggested, he had spoken on behalf of all of the children in Outlandish, and although this was just a little thing in the grand scope of what constituted success, he knew Tallie would be pleased.

Archie kept busy after Tallie left in order to push away the pangs of a lonely heart. He labored over his story until finally, after a few weeks, he had a clever presentation he was satisfied with. He had been working on the illustrations since Tallie had sent him the photographs to use as references for his drawings, and he had already completed a few of them.

He and Tallie wrote to each other often and those letters helped them feel a little less gloomy about being apart. It was the fourth letter Archie received from Tallie, about five weeks after her departure, that sent his mind and heart into a panic.

Dear Archibald,
This letter is a hard one to write, especially since I'm not good at writing like you are, but here it goes.

I'm moving to New Zealand with Gemma . . . for a year.

Now please, before you get too upset, and I know you will, let me explain. First, I do love you and I'm sorry if this hurts you. If you and I were at different places in our lives, I might not go, but we are still both trying to find our way, and I don't want to miss this opportunity.

I promise you, Gemma didn't demand I go, but she did say if I went with her, she would support me and teach me for the entire year. I still have no idea why she would be willing to do that for me, especially since I offer her nothing more than assisting her in menial ways, but for whatever reason she has offered and I do see so many benefits in going.

I've told her I only want to be a photographer, not a photojournalist, and she seems okay with that.

I know you told me not to, but I told Gemma about your book and she gave me the name of an agent she thought might like to take a look at your work. Knowing there was a good chance you wouldn't pursue it yourself, I contacted the agent and told her about you and your project. Archibald, she was excited about it! She said she would get in touch . . . and even mentioned coming to see you in Outlandish. She has a meeting near there and thought she could see you on that trip.

Maybe I've overstepped my boundaries, but after getting to know you, I felt pretty sure you wouldn't make the phone call, and I really believe in your book. So please give her the opportunity to help you. (Her name is Sybil Schofield.)

I wish I had time to come and see you one more time before I go, but it all happened so quickly, at least the part about me going along, so I only have a little time to get ready. We'll be leaving in two weeks (if my passport comes by then).

I know we agreed to write to each other instead of call, and so I am writing, and I'll admit, writing has made it easier to tell you this. Well, at least a little, but I do wish I could hear your voice one more time before I leave.

I will be praying for your success and am looking forward to having my own autographed copy of Archie Underneath.

A year seems a long time, but I think my life will be in a better place when I return and hopefully this next year you will find your success, too.

I will write to you when I get there and tell you where you can write to me. Please keep the letters coming. I don't know what I would do if I couldn't count on your letters.

I won't forget you, I promise.

I love you.
Tallie

Archie couldn't believe what he'd read. Although he'd never felt this version of it, he was pretty sure he was desperately heartbroken, as well as angry and frustrated all at once. On impulse he went for Tallie's phone number, but as he held the paper in his hand, he changed his mind. He knew he couldn't face her, not like that. So what he did instead was crumple the letter and throw it. He wished he could pace the floor, but since he was sitting in his room, he just put his knees up, propped his elbows on them, and rested his fingers in his thick hair.

He sat like that for many minutes trying to decide what to do with Tallie's words, but what he couldn't get past was the anger he felt about the situation, especially toward Gemma Perrelli.

When there was a knock on his bedroom door, Archie didn't respond. He heard his mother say, "Archie? Are you in there?"

He wished he could be alone. He didn't want to talk to anyone, but because he had never deliberately been rude to his mother, he said, "I'm here. Just a minute, please."

Archie tamed his hair, rubbed his face, and went to lean against the wall, hoping to appear normal.

"Come in," he finally said.

She opened the door and said, "I put a letter from Tallie on your shelf. Did you get it?"

Archie nodded but didn't speak because he knew it would give away how he was feeling.

Annella walked in and sat by Archie. "What's the matter?" she asked.

Not able to speak, Archie shook his head.

"Tell me. What's wrong?"

His voice broke. "Tallie's going to New Zealand... for a year."

His mother hadn't expected to hear that. "Why?" she asked with a look of concern.

"To learn, I suppose. Of course, she's going with Gemma Perrelli. I'm sure she felt she had to because of Ms. Perrelli's patronizing manner."

"I don't know," she said. "Tallie doesn't seem like the type of person who would go all the way to New Zealand for an entire year just because she felt pressured to do so. No, Archie," she said shaking her head. "I think she's given it some serious thought and must have a good reason for going."

Archie shook his head. "Mother, you don't understand."

"What don't I understand?"

"We said we loved each other," Archie confessed. "Why would she do that, and then less than two months later, leave me?"

Annella was astonished by his words and yet seemed pleased by them. "You professed your love to one another? Now why didn't you let me in on that little detail?"

His mother's light expression didn't lighten Archie's mood. "I don't know. I guess I was a little worried you and Father might think we were moving too fast. If anyone knows I'm inexperienced in love, it's you two."

"No two love stories are the same, Archie. Anyway, your father and I suspected. You know you never need to keep anything from us."

Archie dropped his head. "I know. I'm sorry."

"Archie, true love won't be separated by one year of dedicated study to one's interests. She deserves that time to learn, don't you think?"

"She deserves the world," said Archie, fighting emotion. "I want her to do what makes her happy, but I just find myself questioning Gemma Perrelli's motives. That woman is not happy, and she seems to want everyone else to be miserable with her. What if Tallie goes away with her and it wears off?"

"If what wears off?" his mother asked.

"Her love for me. What if she decides she doesn't love me?"

Annella put her arms around her son and patted his back gently.

Backing away she said tenderly, "Son, love doesn't just wear off. Have more faith in your love than that."

"But Gemma might be taking her away for that very reason. She knows how hard that will be on us. She never has liked me."

"Nonsense. She would have no reason not to like you, Archie, and regardless of Ms. Perrelli's reasons for asking Tallie to go with her, Tallie is the one that made the decision to go, and I think you need to respect that."

"I do," he said with a sigh. "I guess I'm just not very happy about it. Why does she feel it's a better option than coming back to Outlandish to be with me?"

"How could she? You know Tallie can't afford to live here in Outlandish. You're still at home trying to find success and she's trying to find hers, too. This is a good opportunity for her, Archie. She doesn't want to leave you, but she doesn't have anyone to support her like you do. It's important for her to consider her own future. She can't depend on something that isn't within reach yet."

Archie pulled in a deep breath through his nose, blew it out through his mouth, and turned his head away from his mother. They sat quietly until Annella said, "Sometimes we can't have what we want right when we want it. I know it doesn't seem fair, especially concerning love."

Archie still had his head turned away from his mother, but she saw him wipe his eyes. "Oh Archie. I hate to see your heart break. This isn't the end though. It's just a little bend in the road, that's all. In the letter, did she end the relationship?"

Archie shook his head.

"Did she tell you she loved you?"

Archie nodded.

"Well, see? Think of all of the things that letter could have said and didn't. She's young and trying to secure her future. That's all. You should be proud of her for that."

Archie said quietly, "I know. I just don't want her to go. I wish my life were more established so she wouldn't have to leave. I wish I could give her that security."

"You can't change what is, though," his mother added. "Love just found you before you were entirely ready for it."

"Mother. Are you suggesting I let her go without begging her to stay?"

Annella wrapped her arm around Archie's arm. "I do think you should consider it."

Archie nodded. "I suppose while she's in New Zealand learning photography, I could be here in Outlandish writing . . . trying to convince an agent to take me on . . . and doing an awful lot of praying."

Annella squeezed Archie's arm a little tighter. "Those are good goals, especially the part about praying. It's easy to forget the obvious things when our minds are so wrapped up in trying to figure everything out. If you leave your life in God's hands, Archie, and trust Him to lead you down the right paths, whether things line up in your understanding or not, He will direct you. He's never overlooked you, and He's not about to do it now."

Archie nodded again with more confidence. "You're right. Every single time my heart is involved in a conflict I forget to pray. Why is that?"

"Oh, who ever knows why?" she said. "It's the way of humans, I suppose, but God is always there, waiting for us, when we remember Him. He will always hear our prayers."

"Thank goodness for that," Archie replied. "I really am a mess, aren't I?"

"No. You're not. You're just in love and sometimes that makes it hard to see clearly."

Archie looked at his mother and smiled. "I am in love."

He laughed and for a moment it turned to a little cry. He covered his face with one hand and rubbed it. He didn't remove his hand until he felt he could control his emotions.

"So, we both know what needs to be done, right?" his mother asked.

Archie waited for his mother to tell him.

"You need to dedicate yourself to finishing your book, and you need to do everything in your power to get it published. That way when Tallie comes back, she'll not only *still* be in love with you, but she will be very much impressed."

Archie smiled. "I honestly don't know what I would do without you."

"What are mothers for?"

Annella pulled Archie's face toward her and kissed him on the cheek. "Now I'll let you get to your letter."

"You are always so patient with me."

Annella teased, "Well, when you're a famous writer, you can repay me by connecting me to someone who will publish my cookbook!"

Archie laughed and shook his head. "I would do anything for you, but don't get your hopes up."

"Oh, they are up," she said, giggling.

Annella left the room with a "Ta ta!" and Archie felt much better than he expected to in a mere fifteen minutes of conversation. He pulled out his writing desk and began to pen his letter to Tallie; instead of surprising her with a phone call uttering words of pain and frustration, he would send gentle words of support and encouragement.

Chapter 17

Since Archie was twenty, he was old enough to know that time moved slowly in waiting and rapidly in keeping busy, and so he made plans to work very hard while Tallie was away and hoped to accomplish exactly what she'd entreated him to do . . . or at least give it everything he had. He planned to write some letters to a few agents and see if he might capture the attention of one with his story. He was dead set on refusing help from the agent Tallie had mentioned in her letter, because he didn't want to accept help from Gemma Perrelli. But his father reminded him of his commitment to keep an open mind and that meant if Sybil contacted him, he must be willing to at least talk to her. It was a good thing he came to that resolve when he did, because just six days after Tallie's letter arrived, Sybil knocked on the Plumbys' door.

When Annella opened the door, she saw a tall redhead with dark rimmed glasses standing before her. "Hello," she said with a little question in her expression.

"Hello. Does Archibald Plumby live here?"

"Yes, he's my son."

Putting her hand out the lady said, "My name is Sybil Schofield. I'm an agent with the Camden Street Literary Agency."

Annella was excited when she realized why she must have come, but she was also surprised by two things: first was her English accent, and second was her age. She was much younger than Annella would've expected.

Annella shook her hand. "It's so nice to meet you, Ms. Schofield. My name is Annella."

"Do I detect a British accent?" Sybil asked.

"Yes, and it sounds like you're British as well."

"I am. Where are you from?" Sybil asked.

"Sheffield. You?"

"No way! Really?" Sybil said with her eyes wide. "I was raised in Doncaster, not very far from Sheffield."

"What a small world," said Annella. "Are you living in the States now?"

"Yeah, I am. I moved here a year ago when I was offered a job with the agency. I hope it's okay that I came without calling first. Tallie said I might have more success if I just popped in."

Annella chuckled. "Well Tallie was right and it's absolutely fine. Come in. Archie will be very happy to meet you."

"Oh, does he go by Archie? Tallie used the name Archibald."

"He does prefer Archibald. I'm sure he'll be tickled if you call him that," Annella said.

Annella walked Sybil to the living room and said, "Albert, this is Sybil. She's a literary agent. Come to see Archie."

Albert stood up from his chair, removed his reading glasses and dropped them in his shirt pocket. He walked over to Sybil and put his hand out. "It's nice to meet you, Sybil."

Sybil shook Albert's hand. "Thank you for allowing me to intrude on your evening. I won't be long, I promise."

"You're English, aren't you?"

"Yes, I am," she said with a smile.

Annella showed Sybil a chair. "Please have a seat and I'll just go fetch Archie."

When Annella got upstairs, she knocked on Archie's door.

"Come in."

Annella opened his door. She hunched over and moved toward him. "She's come!" she whispered excitedly.

"Who's come?" he asked.

"The literary agent Tallie told you about in her letter! Sybil Schofield."

"She's here? Now?" he asked.

"Yes. She's waiting in the living room."

Archie seemed a little nervous, so his mother put his mind at ease. "She's an adorable little thing . . . and British, too."

"British?" he asked.

"Yes, from Doncaster. That's very close to where I grew up."

"Is she your age?" Archie asked.

"No, she's very young, not much older than you. Maybe twenty-three, twenty-four."

Archie looked surprised.

"Now hurry up and come down. I'll put on some tea."

"Do you think I should bring my work down for her to see?"

"Not yet. You don't want to seem too eager. Come and meet her first. You can always come back for it when she asks for it."

"Yes, right," he said. "I'll be right there."

Until that very moment, it seemed an impossible dream to Archie. It had never dawned on him it might actually happen. So when his mother left, he couldn't help but smile at the possibility of becoming a published author. But not knowing a single thing about publishing made him nervous as well.

He looked in the mirror to make sure his hair wasn't too out of order, grabbed his umbrella by the door, and exited. When he was down the stairs, he moved to the living room and saw her. Sybil quickly stood and put her hand out to Archie.

"Hello, Archibald. I'm Sybil Schofield, with the Camden Street Literary Agency."

Archie shook her hand. "It's nice to meet you, Ms. Schofield."

"Please, just call me Sybil. I've heard some pretty wonderful things about you and your book. *Archie Underneath*, right?"

"Yes, that's right," Archie said, his voice a little shaky.

"I can see by the umbrella over your head you have truly lived this story of yours."

Archie was trying hard to sound at ease, so he said, "Yes, I suppose I've . . . lived to tell about it."

Sybil laughed lightheartedly. "It's a genius idea to write it as a children's story."

"I can't take credit for it," he said. "It was Tallie's idea."

"And quite a good one!" she said. "I'm certainly captivated by the idea of it. She mentioned you would be illustrating it as well?"

"I am, although I'm not very confident with that part of it."

"Well, we can have a look. There are plenty of willing illustrators if need be."

"That's good to know," Archie said.

"Do you have your work handy? I'm dying to take a peek."

"Yes, I'll just go and get it. Mother, you may serve tea now."

As soon as the words left his mouth, he felt a great deal of embarrassment. Archie had never ordered his mother to do anything. He turned and looked at her with an expression that revealed his shame. Of course, his mother knew he was just nervous and hadn't intentionally been rude, so she said, "Archie, tea is a wonderful idea! Sybil, why don't you come over to the table where Archie can spread his work out for you and you can have your tea."

From the table, Sybil said to Annella, "Tea sounds lovely. I'm feeling knackered after traveling."

From the kitchen, Annella asked, "Where did

you travel from, Sybil?"

"Only from San Francisco, but I'm still not quite acclimated to driving these curvy roads, especially from the wrong side of the car."

"Five hours on those roads can be torture for anyone," Annella admitted.

"I'm afraid it took me seven. And I'm feeling pretty down for it. How long did it take you to adjust to driving over here?"

"I was quite young when I came to the States. In fact, I hadn't even learned to drive yet, so I guess I'm the lucky one."

"Indeed," said Sybil.

Archie walked into the room with his papers, and Annella pushed a little white cart over to the table that held a brightly colored tea set. She said to Archie, "Come and put your stuff here," while she handed Sybil a cup of tea.

"Thank you, Annella," she said, pulling the cup toward her as if it brought her comfort.

Archie put his notebook and a small stack of illustrations on the table in front of Sybil and stepped back. Sybil scooted her chair away from the table, stood with her tea, and backed away. "You know what, I am such a klutz. I think I'd better put my tea aside or we might all regret it."

Annella laughed at Sybil. "Here, let me put your tea on the tray while you look."

Sybil spread out the illustrations—there were six of them—and said, "You shouldn't be insecure about these drawings. They're quite good."

"They are?" Archie asked with relief in his voice.

"Yes, they are. You do plan to give them color though?"

"Yes, those are just my sketches. I was thinking I might use colored pencils. Do you think that would work or would something else be better?"

Sybil squinted her eyes and bit the side of her bottom lip as she considered his question. "Hmmmm. I'm not sure. Do you work with pastels?"

"A little bit," Archie said.

"Would you be willing to put pastels to a couple of them so I can evaluate?"

"I'd be happy to," he answered.

Albert came into the room. "Sybil, what do you think you could do for Archie's book?"

At first Archie was a little embarrassed by his father's direct manner, but because he trusted his business sense much more than his own, he quickly recovered from his doubt.

Sybil shook her head. "Oh, of course. We *should* talk a little about that. Well, I would like to take a look at Archibald's story first, although I'll admit, I'm already sold on the concept or I wouldn't be here. But if it is as I expect it will be, I will make him an offer of representation and hopefully give him the opportunity to get published."

"Is it a very time-consuming process?" Annella asked.

"Usually, but there are a few exceptions," Sybil said. "If several publishers are interested, it may come together rather quickly, but again, that isn't common."

"What is the best-case scenario?" asked Annella.

"What usually takes up to a year might only take a few months if there is a publisher ready to jump on it. There really are so many determining factors. It's hard to say," Sybil said with a little reservation.

"That's what I'm going to be praying for," Annella said, hopefully.

Albert piped up, "Now, let's keep our heads about us. It's always better to assume things won't go so smoothly so there are no disappointments."

Archie hoped it might happen quickly, but because of his inexperience as well as his lack of confidence, he worried Sybil might not like his story after all.

Sybil picked up Archie's notebook and said, "Why don't we back up a little bit and let me take a look at Archibald's story. After that I might be able to make some better projections."

Albert and Annella laughed together over their hastiness. "Of course," Annella said shaking her head.

Archie felt his heart race at the thought of being critiqued by a professional, so he forced a smile in hopes of covering up his anxiety.

"Here Archie, have some tea," his mother said offering him a cup. "Would you like some tea, Albert?"

"No, thank you, dear. I'm going for a glass of Cabernet."

They all sat quietly while Sybil read Archie's story. There were a few moments when she laughed and another when she put her hand to her chest and said, "Aw." Finally when she was done reading she said, "You're a good writer, Archibald."

Archie wished she had said more, but he still smiled and said, "Thank you."

Annella put her hand on Archie's arm and hollered across the room to Albert, who was sitting back in his chair, "Did you hear that, Albert? Sybil thinks Archie is a good writer."

Albert got up from his chair and walked over to the table with his wine glass in his hand. He took a sip and asked Sybil, "What did you think of the story?"

Sybil smiled. "I'm in love with your son's story."

Albert put his wine glass in the air and shouted, "Hallelujah!"

They all laughed together, including Sybil.

Sybil stayed with the Plumbys for an hour. They talked about the agent/author relationship and discussed potential publishers as well as possible offers. At the end of the hour, Archie accepted representation with Sybil Schofield of the Camden Street Literary Agency and agreed to meet her for breakfast, at none other than The Lupine.

Chapter 18

Archie's head was filled with thoughts of being a published author, so sleep didn't come easily that night. Unfortunately when sleep did come, so did the same nightmare he'd had twice before. He was stuck in the sand, watching the monstrous wave, yelling for Tallie to help him. The only variation in the dream was that when she walked away from him with a smile on her face, it made him angry and he began shouting and even cursing at her.

Upon waking, Archie immediately felt shame for his coarse words, especially since he was shouting them at the one he loved. He said out loud, "Lord, where in the world did that come from? Please forgive me."

Archie knew he was still struggling with understanding why Tallie decided to go to New Zealand, but he had no idea there was so much anger bottled up inside of him. It was going to be a challenge to carry on without feeling a bit put out by it all.

He looked at the clock and realized he was, once again, running late. He was getting quite good at that. He rolled out of bed and hurried to the bathroom to shower and get ready for breakfast with Sybil.

Sybil was waiting for Archie in the restaurant. When he walked in, she waved at him and he walked over to the table.

"Good morning," Archie said.

"Good morning to you, Archibald. Eight o'clock came a little soon, didn't it?"

Archie sat down and began setting up his umbrella. "Yes. I'm so sorry."

Sybil watched with interest as he set up his stand, especially since he did it so well with one hand. "You had trouble sleeping, didn't you?" she asked.

When Archie was done with his umbrella, he smiled at Sybil. "How did you know?"

"All my new authors have that reaction," she said. "It's an exciting time in your life."

"It does seem a little like a dream," he said. "I don't think I believed it would ever happen . . . until it did."

"Well, if it makes you feel any better, I didn't sleep, either. I became more and more excited about your story through the night. I'm going to work very hard to find you a publisher, and I really hope your mum's prayers are answered."

"I hope so, too," Archie admitted.

Archie thought of Tallie and her faith in his writing. He felt a little pang of longing and wished it were she who was sitting across from him, but then he remembered that it was because of Tallie he had any chance of success at all and so he decided to embrace this moment with his new agent.

"Are you free the next few days?" Sybil asked.

"Yes, why?"

"I thought I'd stick around if you don't mind. I think a few days together to polish up the story would be good. That way I can begin presenting it to publishers as soon as I return to the office. I'd also like to make a decision about the illustrations before I leave so you can get to work on them. If I have one or two to take with me, that would also help sell the book."

Archie nodded. "Whatever you think is best. I obviously have no idea how this publishing business works."

Sybil put her head down and began to write something in a notebook. When she did, her thick hair practically engulfed her face. She used her hands to tuck it behind her ears, but it fell right back down as soon as she lowered her head again. "Blast! This crazy hair of mine!" She reached into her purse and grabbed a clip. Holding it up she said, "This little clip is a lifesaver!"

Archie couldn't think of a single fitting response, so he just sat quietly.

"Guys are so lucky," she said still trying to fit all of her hair into the clip.

Archie pointed at the curly mass of hair on his forehead and said, "Not always!"

Sybil laughed. "I like your hair. It suits you."

"Thank you. Well... your hair... suits you, too."

When Sybil chuckled at his response, he felt foolish for saying it.

Aware of his embarrassment, she said, "I don't think our hair deserves any more of our attention this morning. What do you think?"

Archie shook his head. "I quite agree, but breakfast..."

"Yeah, let's flag down that waitress," she said.

When they were finished eating and going over some little details of the story, Sybil asked Archie, "How long would it take you to finish one illustration in pastel?"

Archie shrugged. "Probably a full day of work... but maybe just a few hours. It's hard to say for sure. I haven't worked with pastels in a while."

"Do you have some time today? I mean, I don't want to put too much pressure on you, but if I can leave here with an established book idea *and* a sample illustration, it will be much easier to get our creative point across."

"I understand," Archie said. "I have an appointment with the editor at the paper this morning, but it shouldn't take more than an hour or so."

"Why don't you see what you can get done and maybe we can reconvene this evening?"

"That would be fine. What time?" he asked.

"Should we do dinner?" she asked.

Archie was really hoping for a night at home to talk to his parents about everything that had taken place, but he didn't want to be rude, so he said, "Um, sure. Where would you like to meet?"

"Well, I am dying to try your mother's restaurant. Should we meet there?"

"Of course. Six-thirty?"

"Excellent!" she said. "Don't forget to bring along your illustration, even if you don't get it finished. I'm anxious to make that decision."

Archie was at his table when Sybil arrived at Flavors of the Earth. He stood so she could see him. When she got to the table, she said, "So how'd it go? Any luck with the illustration?"

"Well, I finished it, but I'll let you tell me how you think things went." He opened a portfolio, which revealed a pastel illustration inside a clear plastic sleeve, and pushed it toward Sybil. She put it in front of her and sat analyzing it for a moment before saying with a smile, "Yes. Let's do pastel."

"Are you sure?"

"Absolutely. It fits the story perfectly! If you could get just one more done before I leave, that would be very helpful."

Archie wondered if that *one more* would end up being yet one more by the time Sybil left, but he didn't let on that he was thinking that. Instead he said, "I think I can accommodate."

Sybil closed the folder. "Good. So now that I've made a decision for you, it's time for you to make a decision for me."

Archie appeared confused so Sybil laughed and said, "Don't worry, I just want you to help me decide what to eat for dinner."

"Oh, that shouldn't be too difficult. I can recommend, well, I can recommend everything. Do you like fish? Or do you prefer chicken . . . or steak?"

"I love fish . . . and chicken . . . and steak. Actually, I just really love to eat."

Archie laughed at Sybil. "You're not alone in that. Would you believe there isn't one thing on this menu I don't like? And believe me I've tried all of it."

"You must have a lot of self-control though, huh?"

"Why do you say that?" asked Archie.

"Because you're so thin."

Archie shook his head. "Trust me, it's not self-control. I have none of that when it comes to Mother's dishes. It's only a very fast metabolism."

"Lucky you. I have no fast metabolism, but I have wonderful self-control when it comes to broccoli, cauliflower, lima beans . . . and, well, most vegetables. I'll admit they have to be pretty disguised for me to eat them."

"No vegetables?" asked Archie.

"No sir," she said. "I grew up on fish and chips, meat and potato pie, mincemeat, baked beans, and, well, not very many vegetables. I mean, carrots and an occasional serving of peas, but that's about it."

"What a shame. You're missing out on such wonderful flavors."

"To each his own, Archibald."

Sybil ended up ordering a tuna steak with rice, and Archie laughed hard when she substituted an apricot tart for the vegetables.

Annella came out from the kitchen while they were eating and said, "Are you two enjoying your food?"

"Oh Annella, this is delicious! Especially the apricot tart."

"That was *you* that ordered a side of dessert, was it?"

"I can't help it. I loathe vegetables."

Annella shook her head. "I'll bet, given the opportunity, I could change your mind."

"I really doubt it."

"But you're English, dear. You must've grown up on garden vegetables."

Sybil shook her head. "We didn't even have a garden. My mum usually ordered takeout for my sister and me. It was just the three of us, and truth be told, I don't think my mum likes vegetables much either. Ha!"

Annella sat down while they chuckled over the funny conversation. Putting her hand on the portfolio that sat in the empty chair, she asked, "Did you make a decision about the illustrations?"

Archie let Sybil answer. "Yes, we're going with pastels. Archibald is going to try to get another to me before I leave, and then I'll be able to start pitching the book idea to publishers."

"Oh, I'm so excited about it all!" Annella said. "Thank you for giving Archie a chance, Sybil. This is such a wonderful opportunity for him, and I know you'll find him to be hardworking and professional, and you've already seen his wonderful gift with words."

Sybil looked at Archie, but his face was turned toward the piano that was being played on the other side of the restaurant. Looking back to Annella, Sybil said, "He does have a gift and I hope we're not the only ones who will appreciate it in the end."

"Do you think you'll be able find a publisher for his book?"

Sybil nodded and smiled to Annella while Archie was still turned the other direction only mouthing the words, "I think so," which made Archie turn his head back to the table so he could see her response, but he was too late. The exchange was finished.

Annella stood. "So much fun to consider all of the possibilities, but I must get back to the kitchen."

"Thanks for popping out to say hello!"

"Oh, I'll be back out in a little while with a plate of tempting vegetables that you won't be able to resist."

Sybil looked from Annella to Archie. "It's not going to work, you two."

Archie raised his eyebrows. "I think it is."

Sybil did like the vegetables that night and every vegetable Annella brought out for her to try over the next few days when they were at the restaurant, except for Brussels sprouts which she claimed were "much too bitter" for her taste buds.

The book was polished and the illustrations were in the works when it was time for Sybil to go back to San Francisco to begin pitching the book.

Archie walked Sybil to the parking garage. When they stood outside her car he said, "I can't thank you enough for being willing to take a chance on me and my book. It's really boosted my confidence these past few days."

"I don't see it as taking a chance at all. I believe in this book of yours and plan to give it everything I've got to convince a publisher to believe in it, too."

Archie smiled crookedly. "Well, thank you . . . again."

Sybil put her hand out to Archie. He shook it and said, "I guess I'll let you be off. I hope your drive home is a little less harrowing than your trip here."

"I should be fine," she said, looking a little worried.

When Archie turned to walk away, Sybil said, "I've gotten so used to being under your umbrellas, I might just have to get my own." Archie smiled and Sybil said, "I'll tell you what, if I come back with a contract for you to sign, you can help me pick one out. How does that sound?"

"Right. Yes." he said. "I would be happy to."

Chapter 19

Archie received a short letter from Tallie a few days after Sybil left. She was still settling in, but wanted to send the address where she would be living so he could write to her. She promised to write more when she had a little more time.

He wrote back telling her about his visit with Sybil, and thanked her for connecting them, confessing he probably wouldn't have accepted her help if she hadn't shown up on his doorstep. He also admitted he was very excited at the possibility of being published and gave Tallie all the credit for the idea to write the book.

Archie stayed so busy working on his illustrations over the next two weeks that he was surprised when he found another letter from Tallie.

Dearest Archibald,

How exciting to hear that your meeting with Sybil Schofield went so well! Gemma told me she talked to Sybil the other day and that she really believes in your project. I'm anxious to hear how it all pans out, so don't forget to keep me in the loop, okay?

New Zealand is so pretty! I wish you could be here with me. I've never seen such breathtaking views. My photographs are gorgeous (not by my skill but because of the scenery).

Gemma has been different here. Being out in nature seems to agree with her. We've had some interesting talks about life. I think you were right about her. She seems happier away from her hectic career. I wasn't exactly sure why she wanted to come. She only told me she was working with someone on a book, but it seems she just wanted to get away. I'm wondering if I'm here merely as her companion, which is fine with me.

We're staying on Waiheke Island near Auckland. I can't even believe this place exists. You should see this house we're staying in. The entire back wall is made of windows that look out on the ocean. I get to watch all of the "be-bumists" enjoying sunbathing and surfing. By the way, Gemma was so entertained by your family's word invention that we've been referring to ourselves as be-bumists since we got here.

I'll take some photographs and send them to you with my next letter. (People who live like this all of the time are so spoiled. I honestly feel guilty for being here.)

Anyway, I need to run. Gemma and I are getting ready to take pictures of the sunset. She's going to show me what camera settings to use to capture the most realistic tones of the sky. I'm already learning so many new things.

Missing you.

Love,
Tallie

P.S. Can you imagine how good I'll be at beach living after a year of this?

Archie missed Tallie more after reading her letter, but because she seemed happy, he was able to set the letter aside without feeling too miserable over her absence.

He started to reply to Tallie's letter but was interrupted by a knock on the door. His mother was at work, but he knew his father was downstairs, so he let him answer.

A moment later his father hollered, "Archie, Sybil's here to see you!"

"Hm," he said to himself, while putting down his piece of paper. Grabbing his umbrella, he headed out of his room and down the stairs.

"Sybil. I wasn't expecting you."

She went and stood with him under his umbrella and squeezed his arms, a little too tightly, showing excitement. "Archibald! I'm sorry I didn't let you know I was coming, but just wait until you hear what news I have for you!"

Archie immediately felt a little panic attack coming on (even good news could trigger one), so he breathed deeply and managed to say, "What news?"

"Let's sit down. I want to show you something."

"All right," he said continuing to breathe deeply.

When they sat at the table, Sybil said, "Mr. Plumby, why don't you join us? I think you might like to hear this."

"It sounds like news we should pull the missus in for. Should I call her?"

"I'm willing to wait a little bit if you're willing to wait to hear it," she said.

Archie said, "Father, call. She'll want to be here."

Annella was soon coming through the front door. "I'm here!" she called as she walked in.

Albert chuckled. "You're still in your apron, dear."

"Oh goodness," she said as she untied it and took it off.

She quickly sat down at the table. "So what's the news?"

They all sat in anticipation as Sybil pulled out a few pieces of paper and set them out on the table. "Three significant offers," she said.

"Three!" Annella said, laughing.

Albert whooped and patted Archie on the back.

Archie remained quiet, still trying to get through the panic attack, which was getting worse by the minute.

"I think there is an obvious right choice here, but they're yours to choose from. So, I'll just help you understand what each one offers."

They all sat looking at Archie. He wanted to say something but he felt panic, joy, and excitement all at once, so it could only be managed with silence.

Annella grabbed Archie's free hand and said to Sybil, "Don't worry, he's happy. He just needs a minute."

"Archibald, I had a feeling this was going to happen. Publishers seem especially interested when the story is real, because readers are fascinated with real characters."

Annella and Albert laughed as Archie continued to sit in silence.

"So are you ready to hear the offers?"

Archie didn't speak, but Albert did. "Let's hear it!" he said, swooping his fisted arm upward.

"Okay. The first is an offer to publish your book with a very generous advance." When she pointed to the dollar amount, Archie's eyes opened wide and Albert whooped again.

"While it is a large advance for one book, especially for a first-time author, the next offer is even better."

Annella squeezed Archie's hand and examined his face, but it was unchanged.

"This publisher would like for you to make *Archie Underneath* a series of three books, beginning with the one you've already written. As you can see, this advance is quite good too, and the publisher is one authors seem to enjoy working with. But then there's a third offer I'm fairly sure you won't be able to refuse."

Sybil stopped and looked at Archie. "Archibald, are you all right? I know this is a lot to take in."

Archie nodded, but only once, and left his chin down and his eyes up.

She said with a smile, "Are you ready to hear about the third offer or do you need a few minutes?"

Albert laughed and answered for Archie. "He's ready. Tell us, already."

Sybil smiled and nodded. "Okay. This publisher would like a series of *six* books, the first of which they want to rush and have ready for purchase by Christmas. And the advance, Archibald . . . I think you'll be pleased."

She turned the piece of paper toward Archie and pointed at the number. "That's enough to carry you for a while, right?"

Albert and Annella craned their necks to see what number Sybil was pointing to. They looked at each other in shock and turned to look at their son. Archie's face was stark white by now, and he had completely yielded to his panic attack. His chest moved up and down quickly, and he blew out loud breaths from his rounded lips.

"Oh dear," his mother said with a bit of a chuckle. "Let's give him a minute to process all of that and recover a bit."

Archie nodded and breathed out a "Thank you, Mother."

When a few moments had passed and Archie had recovered some pink in his cheeks, Sybil spoke up. "So what do you think?"

Archie didn't say anything at first but eventually breathed in deeply, exhaled and said, "I'm completely overwhelmed. But I might be willing to give it a whirl . . . I suppose."

Albert and Annella broke out into laughter. Sybil smiled. "I thought you might say that. So I think I'll stay in Outlandish for a week or so. They want at least two ideas for content for future books. Maybe we can work that out while I'm here?"

"Yes. That's . . . fine."

"How many illustrations have you completed?"

"Five," he said.

"How many did we decide on?" she asked.

"With four full page spreads, I think we decided on twenty?"

"Yes, that sounds right," she said. "How fast can you get the next fifteen finished?"

"Oh my. I really have no idea."

"Since they want your book in the stores by Christmas, that means you have six weeks to complete your part. So that's fifteen illustrations in a month and a half. Is that even possible for you?"

"Maybe I should quit my job at the paper?"

Sybil answered, "Unless you are very opposed to it, I think that might be a good idea. These six books will keep you very busy for the next . . . oh, I don't know . . . five or six years."

Annella put her hand to her cheek and smiled, "What an exciting day, Archie. I'm so proud of you."

Archie put his hand in his hair and without thinking, he moved his fingers around, so when he took his hand out of his hair, it looked a little wilder than usual.

Sybil couldn't keep herself from laughing. "You could go for that image if you'd like. No one will ever forget you."

Archie, finally able to think clearly said, "What? The umbrella isn't enough?"

They were all amused by his words and laughed heartily.

"Let's celebrate, shall we?" said Annella.

"Do you need to get back to the restaurant or can we celebrate now?" Albert asked.

"I think they can manage without me for a couple of hours. Let me just give them a call to make sure."

"Then dinner is on me," Sybil said. "Where shall we go?"

"I vote The Jazz House," said Albert.

"Oh! I like the sound of that," Sybil said.

Annella came back a moment later. "They're happy to cover for me at the restaurant. Just give me a few minutes to change and freshen up."

The Jazz House was known for their specialty salads and addicting cardamom rolls, but their finest feature was the dance floor. It was the largest dance floor in Outlandish. The Plumbys had never been there to dance, much to Annella's dismay, but Annella did love their blackberry blue cheese salad, and because she was a chef herself, she always took the time to try the dishes of other chefs in Outlandish. She was known for leaving notes on the table complimenting the chef's choice of flavor blends.

While they ate together, Archie's father asked Sybil question after question about the business side of the book deal, and she, being equally sociable and professional, was happy to answer each of his questions. Annella, who was always at work to make sure everyone was relaxed and at ease, interrupted on occasion to ask Sybil about her family and her home in Doncaster. Archie wished he could be as good at on-the-fly conversation as his parents were, but it seemed, just as he had what he considered the perfect thing to say, the conversation moved on. So he sat quietly and enjoyed listening.

Finally when Albert could think of nothing more to ask, he leaned over to Archie and whispered, "I hope you don't mind me asking all of the questions. I just thought I'd try to be useful since this is all new to you."

"Of course. I appreciate it. I don't think I would have thought of one single question to ask."

"Archibald," Sybil announced, "you're very lucky to have such magnificent parents. You can't go wrong with them by your side."

"You are absolutely right and if I do go wrong, it certainly won't be because of them."

The jazz band that had been taking a break returned to the small stage and resumed playing.

"I haven't danced in years," Sybil said longingly.

Archie was not pleased when his mother announced, "Archie dances!" Why don't you take her to the floor, Archie."

The look he gave his mother made her regret her words, "Mother, you know I don't dance in public."

Annella decided to follow through with her idea. "Yes, but I also know that you are a very good dancer and you haven't been brave enough to have any partner other than your mother."

"That's because you are the only one who has learned to dance with a man with an umbrella in his hand."

"That's true," she said, "but it's not too much to learn. You should at least offer to let her try."

Sybil looked at Archie. "Yes, you should. I'm sure we can figure it out. Besides, I'm much too curious now."

Archie rubbed his face, hoping to be let off the hook, but Sybil said, "Ah, c'mon. What do we have to lose? It will be your first public appearance. You must get used to that, you know."

Archie was prepared to decline, and not feel at all bad about it, but his father piped in. "You *did* say you were determined to keep an open mind. Isn't that right?"

"Father! You're supposed to be helping me out."

"I'm sorry, son. The truth is, I'd like to see you strut your stuff."

"Just one dance," Sybil begged.

With some reservation, Archie took his umbrella off of its stand and said, "I can't believe I'm doing this."

The song the band began to play as Archie and Sybil walked to the dance floor was "Cry Me a River." Archie held his umbrella in one hand and offered the other to Sybil. The dance floor wasn't crowded, but because there were a few other people dancing, and Archie didn't want to take anyone out with his umbrella, they agreed not to venture too far from their starting place.

The song began slowly, so they just sort of swayed to the music under Archie's umbrella hand in hand. When the tempo picked up a bit, Archie, suddenly comfortable on the dance floor, because he really was proud of his dancing skills, moved into some more sophisticated moves and even twirled Sybil.

"Very suave," Sybil said.

With an uncharacteristically proud look, Archie said, "Why, thank you."

Sybil laughed and looked over at his parents, who were also laughing at the scene. It wasn't Archie's dancing that made them laugh—no he definitely had the moves. He looked like he belonged there more than anyone else on the dance floor. They only laughed because they were surprised how at ease he was, considering it was his first time dancing in public, and with someone besides his mother.

The tempo slowed again at the very end, so Archie and Sybil finished their dance with simple sweeping movements and eventually went back to the table where Archie set his umbrella back in its stand next to his chair. His parents were clapping for them. Archie suddenly felt very embarrassed by it all.

Archie was thankful their dinner arrived just as they returned to the table so they might have something to do besides discuss their dance. Unfortunately, that dance wouldn't soon be forgotten, even with tempting food sitting in front of them.

"Where did you learn to dance like that?" Sybil asked.

"Mother taught me. Father doesn't dance, so she insisted I learn."

"I do too dance. I just don't do it very well. Archie definitely got those stylish moves from his mother."

Sybil said to Annella, "Then you must take your turn dancing with Archibald after we eat."

"I think that's a marvelous idea," Annella answered.

Archie pouted. "Seriously? Do I have to? I did only commit to one dance."

"But you looked like you were having a splendid time, and it has been too many years since I've been on a real dance floor. With her own little pout she added, "For your ole mum?"

Chapter 20

Tallie and Gemma were having breakfast outside on the deck on a particularly clear, beautiful morning at Waiheke Island when Gemma's phone rang.

"Gemma Perrelli," she answered.

"Oh, hi, Sybil. How are you?"

At the name *Sybil* Tallie's ears perked up.

"It was nothing," Gemma said. "Really, Tallie is the one to thank. She's the one that spotted his talent. I was only helping out a friend."

Tallie and Gemma met eyes and Gemma lifted her chin and smiled. "How is Archie coping? Enjoying it or overwhelmed by it? . . . That's good to hear and when is the release? . . . Oh, it's on the fast track, is it? Well, that'll be good for him. I think first-time authors must get anxious waiting for their work to be in print. . . . Uh-huh. I hope this book goes big—for both of you. . . . Hm. Well, that's an unexpected bonus. . . . Really? I'm impressed. Dancing? I never would've guessed it."

Gemma glanced at Tallie and watched her countenance change.

"Yeah, I liked the Plumbys. Nice people. . . . Yes, well good luck! Nice to hear from you. Bye-bye."

When Gemma hung up the phone, she expected Tallie to immediately ask about the call, but she didn't, so Gemma said, "Sounds like Archie's enjoying the book business."

Tallie turned her head in question and asked, "What was it you were saying about dancing?"

"Apparently Archie's quite the dancer!"

Tallie knew her face and neck were getting blotchy, so she jumped up and said, "Oh, will you excuse me for a minute? I just thought of something I forgot to do."

"Are you all right?" Gemma hollered after her.

"Yeah, I'm fine!" she said from the other room. Tallie went to her bedroom, sat on her bed, and began crying.

Gemma knocked on the door.

"Are you sure you're all right?" she asked.

"I'm fine," she said in a rough voice.

"Tallie, let's talk."

When Tallie didn't answer, Gemma opened the door and walked into the room. "Now what's the matter?" she said while sitting on the bed next to her.

"Did Archie dance with Sybil?" Tallie asked.

"It seems so," she replied. "That bothers you?"

"He wouldn't dance with me," Tallie said through a little sob.

"Oh, I see," Gemma said, patting Tallie's back. Gemma wasn't used to showing affection, so it was a little uncomfortable for both of them.

"I should have stayed," Tallie said sadly. "He told me he loved me and only a few weeks later, I left him. He must have been so insulted by that."

"He told you he loved you?" Gemma questioned.

Tallie nodded.

"Obviously you feel the same way about him?" she asked sounding a little disappointed.

Tallie nodded again.

"Well, just because he danced with Sybil doesn't mean he's in love with her."

"But you don't know Archibald like I do. If he danced with Sybil, there has to be something between them. Besides, he didn't write back to me after my last letter. I knew something was wrong."

"Well, it's a good thing you're here with me then, isn't it? I'll take your mind off of Archie. Who knows, maybe you'll find a man from Auckland. Can you imagine being able to live here? Outlandish is nothing compared to this place!"

Tallie, of course, would rather have been in Outlandish with Archie than anywhere, but she did appreciate Gemma's attempt to raise her spirits, so she lifted one side of her mouth into a mock smile.

Gemma surprised Tallie by leaning over and giving her an awkward hug. While patting her on the back she said, "There are other fish in the sea. It's better that you focus on your career anyway." Unwrapping her arms from Tallie, she put her hands on Tallie's shoulders and said, "Just imagine who you'll have to choose from when you're a successful photographer traveling the world!"

Tallie hoped Gemma's heart wasn't as calloused as it seemed. If she could pick anyone, anywhere, she would pick Archie. Tallie looked down, and Gemma let go of her.

Looking back up Tallie asked, "Did it sound like Sybil had feelings for Archibald?"

Gemma was quiet at first but eventually said, "I'm afraid so. I'm sorry."

Tallie was desperate to know more. "Did she come right out and say it?"

Gemma nodded with reservation.

Tallie put her hands over her face and cried quietly. Gemma slumped her shoulders and frowned.

"Hm," she said. "Well, is there anything at all I can do to make you feel better?"

Tallie shook her head.

"Then I guess I'll leave you to cry it out, but how about we go dancing tonight?"

Tallie shook her head again.

Gemma bent down to meet Tallie's eyes. "No? There are some pretty tempting men on this island."

"No, thank you."

Gemma shrugged her shoulders. "You can't say I didn't try. Well, I'll be out on the deck if you need me."

Tallie decided to write to Archie, but as difficult as it would be, she also decided she wouldn't say anything about Sybil. She wanted to give him the opportunity to tell her on his own.

A week later in Outlandish, Annella was getting ready to leave for work and was running a tad late, so she hollered up to Archie, "Archie! I'm off to work! I put a letter from Tallie on the table for you!"

Archie opened his door and hollered down, "Thank you! Have a nice evening!"

He went down to get the letter and took it to his room to read. Tired from working on illustrations all day, he lay down on his bed.

Dear Archibald,

I've been missing you. Since you didn't write back to me after my last letter, I've been wondering what's keeping you so busy. Is it the illustrations or is it some other book business that keeps you tied up?

Gemma and I sat out on the deck this morning and talked about my career. She's going to connect me with some people who do tour guides and need photographers to travel and take photos for their books. This could take me all over the world. Pretty exciting, huh?

We're thinking of going dancing tonight. The nightlife here is pretty great. We've met all sorts of people!

So do you have a release date for your book? I'm looking forward to having my copy. You'll have to make sure you sign it for me since I'm pretty sure Sybil is going to make you famous.

Speaking of Sybil—does she come to Outlandish much or do you mostly correspond through mail? I'll bet you've been forced to talk on the phone, haven't you? Looks like your life is going to be changing fast. I hope you're ready for it.

Well, I better run. Gemma is waiting for me to join her for a glass of wine. You could even drink here in New Zealand. The legal age is eighteen.

Take care,
Tallie

Archie put the letter on the floor and stared at his canopy deep in thought.

Something isn't right. Is she upset because I forgot to write to her? She didn't even end her letter with Love, Tallie. Dancing? Why would she tell me she was going dancing? Why would she even go dancing? And traveling around the world? She didn't sound at all like herself.

Archie got up and grabbed a piece of paper, anxious to write her back and hopefully clear up anything that might have upset her.

Chapter 21

Confrontation had never been Archie's strong suit, and when he sat down to write to Tallie, he chickened out. He hoped a kind, nonconfrontational letter would elicit an equally light response and that his mind would be put at ease, but three weeks later he was still waiting for her response.

Sybil had gone back to San Francisco telling Archie she would keep in touch as things progressed on the publishing side of things. She didn't say when she'd be back but did encourage Archie to keep busy with his illustrations while she was gone. He was grateful to have something to occupy his time and his mind.

Archie had purchased his usual papers and was on his way to the library to read them. Although he was no longer in need of career direction, it was a routine he enjoyed, so he kept it up. He walked in and waved to Mrs. Pinkers, who was busy with some patrons. When he sat down and opened the *Pacific Coast Buzz*, he saw a photo in front of him that caught his attention. When he looked closer, he realized it was a photograph of him, under his umbrella on the beach. He glanced at the title, *Ten Reasons the Beach Should Be Your Next Getaway*. He quickly looked to see who was credited for the photo and saw Tallie's name. He was surprised by it, especially since she said she wouldn't use any photos of him without permission. He wondered if Gemma had put her up to it.

"Hm," he whispered to himself, "why would she do that?"

Feeling a burst of courage, Archie decided he would go home and write the letter to Tallie he had intended to before. Picking the papers up, he waved to Mrs. Pinkers and walked out of the library.

When he got home, he rushed up to his bedroom, pulled out his paper and a pen, and began writing.

The doorbell rang just as he was getting started, and since he was the only one at home, Archie went to answer the door. When he did, he saw Sybil standing there.

"Sybil. What are you doing here?" he asked.

"There's my umbrella man," she replied.

Archie was getting used to Sybil's extroverted personality, and he did like her, but he wasn't entirely comfortable around her. It was the first time he'd heard her use the term *umbrella man*, and he wasn't sure he liked it very much, especially since she said *my* umbrella man.

"Well, are you going to ask me in?" she asked in a teasing voice.

"Yes. Um. I'm sorry," he said trying to shake off the confusion he felt.

Moving away from the door so she could come in he asked, "Do you have some news or . . . ?"

"No. I've been away for a couple days and thought I'd make a little detour through Outlandish on my way back, just to see how things are going with the illustrations."

"I see. Away on business?"

"Yeah, I signed a new author who lives in Hollister."

"That's good news."

"Yeah, it is. Although I'm not nearly as excited about that author as I am about my umbrella man," she said pointing her finger at Archie and raising her eyebrows.

Archie hoped nothing in his expression revealed the anxiety he felt over her odd behavior. He wondered why she kept referring to him as her umbrella man. She'd never done it before. In order to, hopefully, direct the conversation back to the book, Archie said, "The illustrations are coming along. I should meet the deadline with no trouble at all."

"Perfect!" she said. "May I see them?"

Grateful for the shift in mood, Archie sighed unknowingly and said, "Yes. Why don't I put on some tea while you take a look?"

"Are your parents away?" she asked.

"Father is out of town on business and Mother is at the restaurant."

Sybil seemed pleased to hear that. "Why don't you go ahead and get your drawings, and I'll fix the tea."

Archie was growing more and more confused, but agreed and walked away to gather his illustrations. When he got back downstairs, he put them on the table and said, "Did you find everything you needed?"

"I did," she said. "Let's take a look at your illustrations while the water is heating."

Archie laid them out on the table. He pointed to an illustration that included a living room fort and said, "Do you think the blue in this is too bright?"

Sybil shook her head. "No, not at all. It's brilliant. It may be my favorite one yet. Vivid colors are what make your illustrations pop, Archibald."

Archie let Sybil look at the illustrations, and they talked about each one a little bit. When they were done he said, "I'll just take them back to my room, and we can have tea."

"Is your bedroom ceiling still lowered like it was in the story?"

"Yes, it is."

"Would it be possible to take a peek? I'd love to see it in real life."

Archie wasn't crazy about the idea, but he shrugged a shoulder and said, "All right, but should we have our tea first?"

"Oh, okay," she said.

When they sat down, there was a strange silence. Archie had never felt so uncomfortable with Sybil and didn't quite know what to say. He expected Sybil to carry the conversation like she usually did, but she seemed to be preoccupied.

"Is everything all right?" he asked.

She shook her head like she was coming out of a stare. "Yeah. I'm just knackered from traveling. With all the driving I've done over the past year, you'd think I would be used to it, but it always makes me feel a little out of sorts. Maybe a walk in the fresh air will help. Would you like to walk on the beach with me for a bit?"

"Should we finish our tea first?" he asked.

"You know, I think my stomach might handle it better once I've had a little walk."

"All right," he said.

The wind was a little stronger than usual that afternoon so Sybil had to stop to find her hair clip, and Archie had to keep a hold of his umbrella canopy.

"Too bad I can't use one of those," Archie teased.

"Well, you could if you wanted to," Sybil said, laughing.

Sybil stopped walking so Archie did, too. She took the clip out of her hair, turned, and clipped Archie's hair back from his face.

"There. See how fabulously it works?"

Archie knew he must look ridiculous, so he immediately took it out.

"Oh, c'mon. It looked good," she teased.

"Mm-hm. I doubt that," he said handing the clip back to her.

Sybil took the clip with one hand and quickly grabbed Archie's free hand with the other. He thought about pulling it away but didn't for fear of hurting her feelings. Besides, he wondered if there might be another reason for it that he hadn't had time to comprehend.

"You know, Archibald, I missed you."

Archie, caught off guard by her words, remained quiet.

"Did you miss me?" she asked. "Maybe just a little?"

He hoped she wasn't doing what he thought she might be doing. Pausing to find the right words he cleared his throat and finally said, "Um, I . . . well, I was just so busy working on the illustrations . . ."

Sybil stepped a little closer and said, "I'm really glad we can work together, Archibald. I really like being with you."

Archie's expression proved his confusion. "Um. Are you speaking... from a professional point of view?"

Sybil laughed, let go of Archie's hand and played with his hair.

Archie felt his face turn red.

"Not exactly," she said slowly.

"What point of view *are* you speaking from?" he asked.

"You're so cute when you're nervous," she teased.

Archie finally mustered up the courage to say, "Did I mention that I'm . . . that Tallie and I are . . ."

Now it was Sybil's turn to be embarrassed. "No! You didn't. She didn't, either. Oh goodness. I'm so embarrassed."

"Oh, please don't be," Archie pleaded. "I hope I didn't give the wrong impression . . . Did I?"

"No. You didn't. I'm so sorry. Had I known, I never would have . . ."

Archie looked worried when he asked, "We *can* still work together, can't we?"

Sybil pressed her lips together into a tight smile and shook her head. "Of course we can work together. Oh my. Let's just forget that ever happened. I really am sorry. I had no idea you and Tallie were a couple. She only referred to you as a friend."

Archie smiled and said, "Well, we are friends."

Sybil sighed. "Honestly, I think I'm just a little lonely here in the States and might be trying a little too hard to make those emotional connections."

"That makes perfect sense," said Archie. "I don't know what I'd do if I had to leave Outlandish and start over. But God will provide those emotional connections you desire. Do you ever pray about it?"

"Not really," she answered honestly. "I mean, I know I should. I believe in God and grew up in the church, but I'm much too independent. I seem to want to tackle life on my own. You know what I mean?"

"Yes, I think I understand," Archie answered.

"But I always feel so much better after I pray about things."

"Yes, well, that's some good advice. I'll make it a priority."

Archie smiled.

"May I ask why Tallie is in New Zealand?" Sybil asked. "It must be very hard on you both to be so far apart."

"Yes, I'm finding that to be very true. She's studying photography. Her teacher is Gemma Perrelli."

"Oh, yes, Ms. Perrelli. Did you know I met her in England before I came to the States? She was there doing photographs for . . . I think, a tourism guidebook. We met at the Sheffield music festival. She was actually my connection for this job. I told her I was a literary agent and was interested in working in the States, and she connected me with the owner of the Camden Street Agency. Nice lady."

Not being the hugest Gemma Perrelli fan, but beginning to wonder if he had been a poor judge of character, Archie said, "She certainly has connections, doesn't she? Evidently I have her to thank for this opportunity, at least in part."

"Yes, that's true, and believe me, I'm as grateful for the connection as you are, Archibald. I know I'm still new in this business, but I've never been so excited about a book. Or should I say, books."

Archie said, "Books. Yes. My mind still can't quite comprehend it."

"You deserve it," she said. "I'm just glad I'm the one who snatched you up."

While Archie did want to be successful and loved the idea of writing for a living, he couldn't quite shake what had just happened with Sybil, so his response was less than enthusiastic.

"I don't know," he said.

"Please don't feel bad about what happened before," Sybil implored.

"I really hope I didn't do something to give—"

"No. Archibald, you didn't. Really, let's just forget it. Please?"

"Are you sure?" he asked. "I don't want to seem ungrateful for all you're doing for me. I'm entirely indebted to you."

"No, you're not," said Sybil. "You are a talent that I am privileged to work with."

Archie knew the feelings left from the awkward exchange wouldn't resolve in this same outing, so he made the decision to let it go and hoped, in time, it would take care of itself. "Well, thank you, Sybil," he said with a smile.

Sybil, intent on changing the atmosphere, said as cheerfully as possible, "Now how about that tea?"

Chapter 22

December came quickly. Archie never did ask Tallie about the photograph. She had been so different in her correspondence that he worried it would only make things worse. They continued writing to each other, but in each letter, Tallie seemed more distant and even a little resentful. They were both obviously suspicious of one another, but neither quite had the courage to come right out and ask or confess anything. Archie continued to sign his letters with "Love, Archibald," but Tallie had quit using the word completely and was closing her letters with phrases like "See you later" and "Cheers," which was frustrating to Archie.

This created a little bit of a dilemma for Tallie when Gemma decided to go home for the holidays.

Tallie would have happily stayed on the island through the holidays, but Gemma seemed more at peace with her life and really wanted to visit her family, so she insisted Tallie go home and visit family as well. What Gemma didn't know was that Tallie didn't have any family to go to. Besides her unplanned confession of her love for Archie, they'd only spoken of lighthearted matters.

Tallie, of course, wanted to go to Outlandish to be with Archie for the holidays, but she was worried she'd show up and interfere with something he hadn't had the courage to share with her; however, there was a small chance she was mistaken about what she had speculated about, and she didn't want to miss out on spending the holidays with Archie if she *was* mistaken. So she scheduled her travel and decided to show up quietly in Outlandish and observe for a while before announcing her arrival. If she was wrong about everything, she would probably discover it pretty quickly and be able to surprise Archie, but if she was right, she would just leave quietly and spend the holidays with Patrice.

She booked her stay in Outlandish for the entire month and would arrive in Outlandish on December 4, which was the day before Archie's first book signing.

The day she arrived, she checked into The Lupine and planned to disguise herself with a hat and sunglasses while observing the town's (and Archie's) activities from a distance.

Tallie had never met Sybil and had no idea what she looked like, so when she walked past her on her way into The Lupine, she greeted her with "Hello" and kept walking.

When she went up to her room, she planned to put her clothes away, freshen up, and head down to the hotel restaurant to get a bite to eat before deciding on her plan. She did get her clothes put away, but after putting her suitcase in the closet, she fell onto the bed exhausted from traveling and before long, she was sound asleep.

Three hours later Tallie awoke and looked around the room trying to figure out where she was. Once she was awake enough to remember, she sat up and rubbed her face. Her first thought was of Archie, her second of her stomach. She couldn't believe how hungry she was.

Looking at the clock, she said out loud, "My gosh! I slept forever!"

She freshened up, changed her clothes, and left the room to get some dinner. When she stepped off of the elevator she saw Archie and gasped. He was walking under his umbrella toward the restaurant. She considered abandoning her plans and running to him, but she couldn't help but wonder what he was doing there. She stayed back but peeked inside the restaurant through an opening in the wall. She watched him walk to a table and set up his umbrella stand. While she stood there watching, someone rushed past her and knocked into her purse.

"Excuse me," the redheaded lady said, turning her head for only a moment.

Tallie didn't even have time to respond because the lady rushed off so quickly.

Tallie stayed back out of sight and continued watching Archie through the opening in the wall. Moments later, she saw the same lady who had just rushed past her walk up to Archie. She bent down to see him under his umbrella and said hello.

Tallie barely heard the words, but she was pretty certain the lady called him "Archibald" and that made her heart drop, not knowing whether it was a sign of affection or merely a formality.

Tallie watched the lady grab both of Archie's hands and dreaded what might come next. Knowing Archie was shy, she expected him to pull his hands away but instead he smiled at her in a way that seemed much too easy for him.

Turning away for a moment she tried to talk herself out of what she was feeling, which was utter fear. Her throat tightened so she swallowed to relieve the pain. Wiping away a tear with determination, she looked back hoping to be able to interpret the situation with less emotion and more logic.

Archie seemed to be watching eagerly as the lady pulled something out of her bag. When she put it on the table, he put his hand on his forehead and smiled again unreservedly. Tallie knew it was Archie's book and understood the lady must be Sybil. This little realization made her feel even worse.

Tallie watched him turn the pages of the book with joy she'd never seen on his face. She thought Sybil watched him with too much fondness for a mere business relationship. She carefully observed Archie's face and gestures and couldn't quite tell if he was only happy about the book or if there was more to his cheery mood.

She sat there watching them for a few minutes until someone asked, "May I help you?"

Feeling she'd been caught doing something forbidden, she quickly said, "Oh no. Thank you. I just realized . . . I forgot something."

She quickly turned to go back to her room where she could pull herself together. She'd just have to order room service.

Archie and Sybil stayed in the restaurant for the next hour discussing the events that were going to take place. Since he wasn't willing to fly, Sybil planned to drive Archie to a few book signings in the San Francisco Bay area. They were scheduled to leave on December 7.

Tallie walked back into her room and stood right inside the door. She didn't even put her purse down. She was angry. She crossed her arms and began talking to herself.

"He said he loved me. How could he so quickly fall for someone else?"

As if suddenly struck with conviction she slumped her shoulders and said, "I can't be too upset. We didn't exactly commit to each other, and I *was* the one who left."

She dropped her purse onto the floor, walked to the bed, and fell face first onto it. She lay there for a minute then turned over onto her back. Putting her hands on her head, she continued talking to herself.

"No matter what," she said with determination, "our friendship shouldn't be conditional, even if he does have feelings for someone else. I knew when I left that anything could happen. It's my fault."

She stood and put her hands on her hips once again feeling furious. "But if he's so fickle to forget me so soon, maybe he's not who I thought he was!"

Suddenly recalling his gentle manner, she softened. "But I was his first romance. Maybe he just got it wrong. It's not exactly his fault if he thought it was love.

"But maybe it is love. Maybe I'm the one that has it all wrong. Maybe they really are just friends."

Tallie was glad she was alone. She knew if anyone heard her they would think she was insane with her extreme trails of thought.

Dropping down to the floor she sighed and shook her head. "He isn't that relaxed around people. He must have feelings for her. I saw the way he smiled at her."

Standing back up, she walked to the mirror and stared into it for a few minutes. "You, Tallulah Z., are an idiot. If you would have stayed, none of this would have happened."

She was finally done talking to herself, but she wasn't done crying. She stood at the mirror and watched herself cry for a full ten minutes then decided to call for room service.

She ordered much too much food to consume in one meal, but she didn't care. She needed to eat for more than nourishment that night. She needed to eat for comfort and she hoped to find temporary solace in the New York cheesecake she ordered two slices of.

Archie and Sybil left the restaurant and went back to his house. His mother was off work and had set tea out on the porch for all of them to have together.

"Hello, you two!" said Annella, putting the tea tray down on the table.

Archie walked over and set the book on the table next to the tea tray.

Annella grabbed it up and said, "Oh my goodness! Look at it!"

"I had it sent to me at The Lupine and it was here when I arrived today," said Sybil.

Albert, who sat smoking his pipe off in the corner, set it down and walked over to Annella. Being a little ornery, he snatched the book out of her hands.

"Oh Albert!" she scolded.

Albert laughed and read out loud, "*Archie Underneath* by Archibald Plumby!" He grinned from ear to ear, handed the book back to his wife, and took Archie into a fatherly hug under Archie's umbrella. When he stepped back he held Archie's arms in his hands and said, "Didn't I tell you there would be something right around that corner?"

"You did, Father, and it presented itself rather quickly, didn't it?"

Albert welled up, which was unusual for him. "Yes, it did, Son."

Archie wasn't used to seeing his father cry, and he felt a sudden rush of emotion.

Annella stepped forward with her own tears, but that wasn't too unusual for her. She took Archie's face in her hands and said, "I am so proud of you! I always knew that umbrella would lead you somewhere wonderful."

Archie kissed his mother's cheek and looked over at his father (who was still struggling with emotion). "If it hadn't been for your and Father's faithful advice and encouragement none of this would have ever happened. I love you both so much."

Annella hugged Archie, and in a valiant effort to gain composure said quickly, "Now let me have a closer look at that book of yours."

They all sat together drinking tea, talking about Archie's future, and eating Annella's delicious, raspberry and white chocolate scones.

Chapter 23

Tallie woke up the next morning with swollen eyes. She was grateful to be all cried out, but still felt miserable. She had hoped to spend the month with Archie, walking on the beach and reminding him of her love for him. She wanted to congratulate him over and over on his book and buy copies for everyone she knew, but instead she decided to leave Outlandish without seeing Archie at all. She knew she was giving in to her fear. She also knew there was a small chance she was wrong about things, but above all, she was afraid of being rejected.

Ultimately what helped her make this decision to leave was her love for Archie. Everything was going so well for him, and she didn't want to taint his joy by asking him to think of her, especially when his affections seemed to have been transferred to the one who had made his dream of becoming an author come true.

She made the decision to go back to Portland and write to him in a couple of weeks. She wouldn't mention she'd been in Outlandish. She wanted to do everything in her power to let him off the hook. She knew it wasn't his fault. She reminded herself over and over again that she was the one who left. She had subjected both of them to the possibility of finding someone else.

She called her mom's friend, Patrice, to see if she could spend at least some of the holiday with her. She knew it would be too hard to be alone, especially considering the circumstances.

Tallie made a plan to leave Outlandish the next day. She was so tired from her long trip that the thought of getting back on an airplane without at least a day to recover sounded like more than she could handle. Of course, being in Outlandish, and apparently staying in the same hotel as Sybil, she would have to be careful. She knew there was a big risk of running into Archie and his parents if she left the hotel, but she also knew part of recovering from her trip would require she spend some time outdoors, so when she went out to get lunch, she wore a low hat and quickly scanned the area before stepping outside.

After purchasing her pretzel and latte, she sat down by the fountain to eat. She couldn't help but wish Outlandish were her own hometown. Not only was it a charming place with so many unique things to see and places to go, but she had also built some wonderful memories she would never forget. Everywhere she looked reminded her of Archie.

When she was finished eating her pretzel, she decided to take a stroll on the beach, but when she stood up to throw her wrapper away, she saw Luke Pindabrook walking toward the fountain. She had only met him a couple of times and didn't expect him to recognize her, but she felt her heart go into a panic when he seemed to quicken his pace toward her.

When he was close enough, he said, "Hello," but she didn't respond. She just turned to walk away.

He hollered "Hey! Tallie, is that you?"

She pretended she didn't hear him and kept walking. She had no idea where she would go, but she really hoped he wouldn't follow her.

When she had walked all the way out of the circle and into a little neighborhood, she finally looked back and was very glad to see he wasn't behind her.

She sat on a curb and finished her coffee hoping he would be gone when she returned to the hotel.

It was the day of Archie's book release, and he was attending his very first book signing. It took place at the dinner theater, and a surprisingly large number of the residents of Outlandish stood in two lines. One line was for those purchasing Archie's book. The other was for those waiting to have their book signed. Because everyone wanted to talk to Archie, the line that he was at the end of was longer and moving much slower.

The theater was decorated with a colorful display of umbrellas, because Archie's publisher thought it represented the book's theme in an appropriately fun way, and Archie sat underneath an extra-large, orange umbrella with the title of his book printed on it. While Archie certainly wasn't comfortable with all the attention, he was enjoying himself. Sybil didn't sit with him, but instead walked around visiting with the people who came to see Archie.

Flavors of the Earth catered the event with a beautiful display of hors d'oeuvres, so people also stood around in little groups eating while they visited with each other. Albert and Annella were proud of their son's achievements and moved around the room thanking people for coming and sharing this special day with them.

Luke had already come by to support Archie and had secured his own copy of *Archie Underneath*, so Archie was surprised to see Luke walk back into the theater. Luke, of course, had come back to tell Archie about Tallie, but every time he leaned over to talk to him, someone would step up and steal his attention, so Luke would step back and wait. This happened over and over again.

Sybil watched this from the other side of the room for a little while and eventually came to Archie's rescue. "May I help you with something?" Sybil asked Luke.

Luke said, "Oh, I was just waiting to talk to Arch."

"Would it be too much trouble for you to wait in line? I would hate to upset those who have been waiting."

"I waited in line earlier. I just had something kind of important to tell him, so I was hoping I could grab his attention for a minute."

"Are you a friend of Archibald's?"

"Yeah, we've been friends since we were . . ." Luke put his hand out to show that they'd been friends since they were little.

"Oh, how nice," she said with a warm smile. She put her hand out. "I'm Sybil Schofield, Archibald's agent."

Luke shook her hand. "I should have known! He told me his agent was from England."

"Yes, Doncaster. I moved to San Francisco about a year ago."

Luke pointed at Archie. "You're very lucky to be working with that guy right there. He's been

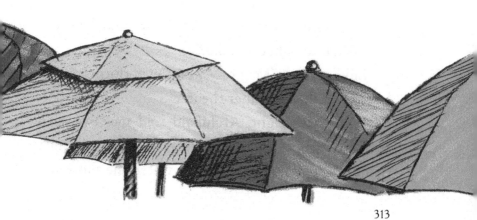

telling me stories my whole life. He was definitely meant for this."

"You wouldn't happen to be the friend he mentioned in the book, would you?"

"Of course I am," he said.

He walked over to a table and picked up a book. He opened it to the illustration of Archie and his black-haired friend, and held it next to his face. Lifting his chin he said, "See the resemblance?"

Sybil laughed. "Actually, I do!"

"I still think he should've used my name so there would be no doubt."

"We talked about that! He tried to use your name, but it just didn't fit with the text. At least he didn't *change* your name to fit the text better. He did consider it."

"You're kidding . . ."

"Yes, actually I am kidding.

"So you're Luke then?"

Luke offered his hand. "Yes. Luke Pindabrook."

"What do you do, Luke?"

Luke smiled. "Magic. My family performs on the beach and in the dinner theater."

"Oh, that's right. Archibald told me. I've seen your family perform from a distance, but just haven't had the opportunity to actually watch the show yet.

When do you perform next?"

"Today at four," he said. "In fact, every day at four, and Saturday evenings, right here in the theater."

"Well, I'm going to come and see you today. It will be a nice little break from all of this book business." She smiled a little sheepishly and said, "Not that I don't love the book business, but this was one of those deals that went really fast and it's completely done me in. A magic show is just what I need."

"How about I pull you in as a volunteer. Are you up for that?" Luke asked.

"Sure! What do I have to do?"

"Just follow my lead."

"Oh no. Is that all I get?"

"When we put the tent over your head and begin throwing things at you, you just say things like, 'Ouch! Stop!'"

"Oh no. That sounds a little dodgy."

"I promise, it'll all be in good fun, and you'll come out looking just as attractive."

Sybil raised her eyebrows at his compliment.

Luke went on. "Do you eat? Because if you do, we could have dinner after the show."

"Actually, I quite like eating and that does sound lovely."

"Yes, *lovely*," Luke said teasingly in a mock British accent, but Sybil didn't catch his meaning and looked at him blankly.

"I'm sorry," he said. "This English accent of yours is killing me. I mean . . . I really love it. You sound a lot like Mrs. P."

Sybil laughed. "Mrs. P? Archie's mum?"

"Yeah. I've called them Mr. and Mrs. P. since I was a kid."

"They're wonderful people," said Sybil. "And it's been great meeting another Englishwoman in America." Realizing she'd been distracted much too long, she said, "You know, I really should be getting back to Archibald's guests."

"Oh, sure," Luke said taking a step backward. "I need to get ready for the show anyway."

"Cheerio!" she said before turning to leave.

Luke smiled and said in a mock accent, "Cheerio!"

Sybil shook her head at his teasing.

"Sorry," he said walking away, completely forgetting why he'd come to see Archie, "I can't help myself!"

At four o'clock Archie went home exhausted after the book signing. Knowing he had some long days ahead of him with the upcoming book tour, he decided to take a nap. Sybil, on the other hand, suddenly energized by meeting a certain dark-haired magician, went straight to the beach to catch the magic show.

Not only was Sybil captivated by the show but was also quickly becoming charmed by Luke Pindabrook, whom she found glancing her direction many times during the performance. About halfway through the show, Jeremiah Pindabrook,

Luke's father, asked for a volunteer from the audience. Luke, decked out in his show clothes, walked in the sand through the small crowd in search of his volunteer. About half of the crowd stood for the show, and the other half sat in the chairs. Luke walked between the people and around the chairs and eventually made his way back to the front row where Sybil was sitting. When he put his hand out to her, she took it and let him lead her up front.

While she usually liked attention, she suddenly found herself a little shy and said quietly, "I changed my mind. Fetch another volunteer."

Luke, used to crowds and loving attention, couldn't imagine not enjoying being up front, so he really was unsympathetic to her plea and only shook his head. "You'll be fine."

"That's rubbish," she whispered with a half terrified smile.

Once in front, Luke announced, "People of Outlandish, let me introduce you to the Englishwoman from . . ." He whispered, "Where is it you're from?"

"Doncaster," she whispered a little impatiently.

"Oh yes. People of Outlandish, let me introduce you to Sybil, the Englishwoman from Doncaster!"

She turned red and smiled as the crowd clapped for her.

"Sybil from Doncaster has informed me she doesn't really want to be up here, so I'm going to make it easy for her."

Two of Luke's brothers brought over a seven-foot long, lightweight, tubular tent. They walked around revealing the hollow construction to the audience.

Luke announced to Sybil as well as the audience, "Sybil of Doncaster, please, do not move. Stand very . . . very still." He then whispered in Sybil's ear, "Remember what I told you to do."

Sybil froze and his brothers put the tent over the top of Sybil so that all the crowd could see was the covering.

"Does that make it easier to be up here?" he hollered from outside the covering.

"Yes. Thank you," came her muffled voice.

Luke said to the audience in a British accent, "Sybil said yes, thank you."

The crowd laughed at him.

At least eight of the members of the Pindabrook family surrounded the narrow tent and began throwing random items over the top. A banana went in as well as a telephone, a small suitcase, a pair of shoes, and many other random items.

From inside the tent, came little noises of discomfort.

"Oh!"

"Ouch!"

"Stop that!"

The crowd oohed and awed and put their hands to their mouths.

Eventually, when at least fifteen items had been thrown into the tent, Luke said, "Sybil from Doncaster, are you well?"

"Yes . . . yes, I believe so!"

"Are you ready to be set free from the tent?"

"Please."

"What is that, Sybil of Doncaster?"

"I said, yes! Please!"

Quickly and dramatically, Luke and a brother grabbed a hold of the tent and threw it off of Sybil. Sybil stood there smiling, deciding she liked volunteering after all, and the audience broke out in applause because not only was Sybil perfectly fine (after being pelted with the likes of fruit and telephones), but there was not one item inside the tent with her. Everything had disappeared.

Luke showed the audience the open ends of the tent and said in his best British accent, "The British *are* known to eat some pretty unusual things."

The crowd roared with laughter, as did Sybil from Doncaster.

After the show was over, Luke hurried over to Sybil. "So how did you like the show?"

"I loved it! Your family is fantastic! But I must know . . . that little trick you did with me in the tent. How did you do it?"

"Ah, I cannot tell you. I'm sworn to secrecy. Family pact."

"That hardly seems fair. I didn't even get to see it."

Luke said, "Then you'll just have to come to the next show and see if you can figure it out."

Sybil narrowed her eyes. "Hm."

"Let me just run home to change before we go to dinner. Meet you back here in fifteen minutes?"

"You must live close!" she replied.

"Yeah, that's our house over there," Luke said pointing to a house so large it looked like a five-star hotel.

"Goodness! You live in that mansion?"

"Well, there *are* eighteen of us."

"I thought Archibald said there were fourteen children. Wouldn't that make sixteen of you?"

"Yes, it would, but two of my brothers are married and their wives live with us now."

"Oh, well, they might as well, as gigantic as that house is."

"The more, the merrier," he said through laughter.

"Do their wives perform with you?" Sybil asked. "I don't think I saw them up there today. Did I?"

"No, but they might someday. It takes a while to learn the ropes. The rest of us have been at it our whole lives."

Sybil shook her head. "I don't think I could ever learn it. It's truly an art form."

"I'd like to think so," Luke said with a large smile.

"Well, it was a brilliant show. No wonder you're so popular around here."

"Thank you," he said. "We have ourselves a lot of fun, but it's a lot of work keeping it interesting. We have to change the show twice a year, and that means coming up with a lot of new material. But it's what the Pindabrooks do!"

"Well, you do it very well."

"Thank you," he said, tipping his ragged top hat. "I'll hurry!"

"Don't worry, I'll be here," she said, waving him off.

Even with the commotion of the crowd behind her, Sybil was lost in thought. She knew she was feeling something she'd never felt before, and she suspected she was quickly falling for Luke Pindabrook.

Chapter 24

Luke and Sybil spent five hours at The Jazz House: Thirty minutes eating, three hours talking, and the rest of the time dancing. That would have made a nice first date, but when they left there, they wandered to Central Circle for coffee and strolled the streets until 2:00 a.m., which meant Luke was very tired when he woke the next morning.

All of the Pinderbrooks were late sleepers, including Luke, so when he opened his eyes and realized it was only 8:00 a.m., he assumed he would fall right back to sleep. However, his mind went directly to Sybil and sleep never came. He lay there with a smile on his face as his mind recalled their evening together.

He probably would have lain there for another hour just like that except a vision of Tallie interrupted his dreamy thoughts, which made him jolt out of bed.

"Oh no! I'm an idiot!"

He had a gut feeling Tallie had no intention of letting Archie know she was there, even though it made no sense to him. Because of that, he worried he'd really screwed up in forgetting to tell him he'd seen her. He hoped he wasn't too late.

When he knocked on the Plumbys' door, not even thirty minutes later, it was Albert who answered.

"Morning, Mr. P! I'm sorry to come so early but I need to talk to Arch. Is he up and around yet?"

He held the door open for Luke. "He is. He's having his breakfast."

Luke walked in and Albert asked, "How's your family?"

"We're all good! Just keeping busy, you know."

"That's good to hear," Albert replied. "Busy is always good."

When Luke walked into the dining room, he expected to find Archie under the dining table, but he was actually eating breakfast under an umbrella at the table.

"Have you graduated to the tabletop?" Luke asked when he saw Archie.

"I guess I have," Archie said looking a little proud of himself.

Luke opened his mouth to tell Archie about seeing Tallie, but Archie spoke first. "I saw you talking to my agent yesterday at the book signing. You looked quite smitten."

Luke's smile revealed he certainly was smitten. "She came to the show yesterday . . . and then we had dinner . . . and we danced . . . and had coffee . . . she's incredible, Arch."

Archie smiled and lifted his chin in mock pride. "Who would've thought it would be me who would bring a woman into your life?"

Luke grinned. "Yeah, I guess, in a roundabout way, it *was* you. Seriously though, Arch, I think she might be the one. I know it was just one evening, but I have this feeling."

"You don't have to convince me. I'm a believer."

"Oh man! I almost forgot, *again*! Stop interrupting me, Arch."

"What?" Archie asked.

"Well, yesterday, when I was trying to get your attention at your book signing, it was because I saw Tallie."

"You saw Tallie?"

"Yeah. I wasn't sure it was her at first. She was wearing a big hat and sunglasses, but when I tried to get her attention, she took off. It was really weird."

"It couldn't have been Tallie. She can't be *here*. She's in New Zealand. And why would she run from you? That's not like her."

"No, I'm pretty sure it *was* her, Arch, and I don't think she wanted me to see her."

Archie felt somewhere between panicked and excited.

"Why didn't you tell me yesterday?"

Luke lifted his hands and carried a guilty expression. "Like I said, that's why I came to see you, but you kept getting interrupted, then I started talking to Sybil . . . and got completely lost in the conversation. Before I knew it, it was time to prepare for the show. Man, I am really sorry."

"Why would she come to Outlandish without telling me?"

"I don't know, man. That's why I thought you should know."

"Where did you see her?" he asked.

"Outside The Lupine, at the fountain. She was eating a pretzel."

Archie grabbed his umbrella off of his stand and stood up. He put his hand on Luke's arm and said, "Thanks, Luke. I need to find her."

"No problem. I hope you do."

After Archie ran out the front door, Annella offered Luke breakfast, and he happily accepted.

Archie didn't run, but he walked as fast as his legs would go. It was only a few blocks to The Lupine, but to Archie it felt like miles. When he finally got to the hotel, he put his head down, closed his umbrella just enough to get through the door, and then opened it again once he was inside.

He hurried to the front desk and was out of breath when he asked, "Good morning, Mrs. Collin. Could you please see if Tallie Greenleaf is checked in?"

The gray-haired lady at the front desk was someone Archie had visited with on a few occasions when he'd come to meet Sybil for breakfast. She was talkative and kind and he enjoyed chatting with her, but all he could think of was finding Tallie.

"Oh hello, Archie," she said much too slowly. "It was a good turnout yesterday, wasn't it?"

"Yes, much better than I expected. Thank you for coming."

"It's just wonderful having a real author in Outlandish!"

Archie didn't want to be rude so he said, "Well, thank you. I am quite happy about it myself." He put his hand on the counter and looked at her pleadingly, "I'm so sorry to rush you, but would you please check your register for Tallie Greenleaf. I'm in a bit of a hurry."

"Of course, I would be happy to. Is she a friend of yours?"

"Yes," he said, "she is."

Mrs. Collin turned her back to Archie and looked through some papers on the back counter. "When did she arrive?" she asked.

"I'm not sure."

While she looked through a stack of papers, she said, "I bought two of your books for my grandchildren. Abel is three, and Cassie is five. I know they'll just love the story!"

Archie sighed without realizing it, and Mrs. Collin turned around to look at him. "Is everything all right, dear?"

Archie covered up his anxiety with a forced smile and said, "I just really need to find Tal—my friend."

Mrs. Collin put her chin down, smirked, and raised her eyebrows. "Oh, I seeee!" she said nodding slowly.

Archie felt frustrated with the kind woman but had no idea how to make her work faster, so he decided to play along and said, "Yes, well, I would really love to find her. She's pretty special to me."

Mrs. Collin, seeming pleased to have been invited into Archie's love story said, "You just wait there for a minute, dear. I'll see what I can find out for you."

When she walked into the back room, Archie found himself feeling incredibly impatient, but he knew there was nothing else he could do, so he stood and waited, tapping his fingers on the counter as he did.

Finally, after about five minutes, Mrs. Collin came back in and said, "I'm sorry, Archie, but she checked out about thirty minutes ago."

Archie dropped his head. "You're kidding?"

"I'm sorry, dear. I just got here right before you came in. Thomas was here when she checked out."

Archie stared at the underside of his umbrella while he tried to figure out where she might be. He finally said, "Thank you, Mrs. Collin," and hurried out the front door.

Now Archie ran—toward the parking garage.

When Archie got there, he ran through the entrance and saw a taxi driving away through the exit. He bent over to catch his breath feeling certain he'd missed Tallie by only a few moments, then stood, cursed, and kicked the concrete wall beside him.

He turned to lean against the wall, put his head down, and sighed.

"Did Archibald Benjiro Plumby just curse?"

Archie looked up quickly but didn't see anyone. "Who's there?" he asked.

"Who else knows your middle name?" came a voice from the outside of the exit.

He turned in a circle and finally saw the top of a hat on the other side of an opening in the concrete wall. He walked over to it and said, "Tallie, is that you?"

She stood and turned to look at him with a look that expressed a little guilt. "Yes. It's me," she said quietly.

Archie ran out of the garage and stood before her.

"What on earth are you doing here?" he asked. "More importantly, why are you leaving?"

Tallie sighed and took off her hat. "I'm sorry, Archibald. I came . . . to see you, but . . ."

"But?" he questioned impatiently.

Tallie put her head down and moved one foot back and forth for a moment. "I know things have changed between us."

"Why have things changed, Tallie? Your letters have been so unusual over the past couple of months. Please don't tell me you've met someone."

"No," Tallie answered quietly.

"Then what?" Archie asked. "I've perceived anger in your letters, and you even posted a photograph in the *PC Buzz* without first asking for my permission as you said you would. That's not like you."

Tallie kept her head down. "I only did that so you would think of me."

Archie lifted her chin with his finger. "Tallie, look at me." Tallie looked up at Archie and he said, "I'm always thinking of you."

Tallie kept her head up but turned her eyes away and said, "I heard Gemma on the phone with your agent and she said you had gone dancing together." She finally looked at Archie and said, "You wouldn't even dance with me."

"Tallie, I can explain."

Before he could continue, she added, "I saw you at the restaurant in The Lupine, too."

"You saw me there and didn't come to me? Tallie?"

"You were with *her*," she said sounding a little annoyed.

"Yes, Tallie. She's my agent. I've been with her a lot over the past few months. Remember, it's you who sent her to me."

He stood staring at her, waiting for her to reply.

"Well, you just seemed so happy to be with her and I thought maybe . . ."

"Maybe what?" Archie asked. "I'm so confused. What are you accusing me of?"

"Well, I did leave, and I shouldn't have expected you to wait for me. I mean, I thought you would, but I shouldn't have expected . . ."

Archie took Tallie's hand. "Tallie, I'm desperate to know what you're trying to tell me. Please just say it."

Tallie hesitated and finally said, "I just want you to be happy. If you've fallen in love with Sybil, it's okay. I understand."

Archie laughed. Feeling a great sense of relief, he said with a wide smile, "Fallen in love with Sybil?"

"What's so funny?" asked Tallie with a little irritation.

"Sybil is my agent, Tallie. I'm *not* in love with her. I'm in love with *you*. How could you even think that?"

Tallie felt her chest get heavy and she let herself cry. "You're not in love with Sybil?" she managed to say through little sobs.

Archie didn't answer Tallie. Instead, he put his palm gently against her cheek and leaned down to kiss her. When his lips met hers, Tallie didn't resist but kissed Archie back as tears ran down her cheeks.

Their kiss was tender but long, and when their lips finally parted, Archie smiled at Tallie and wiped her tears away with his hand, one cheek at a time.

"I could never love anyone but you, Tallulah Z. Greenleaf. Haven't I convinced you of that?" Dropping his head to the side, he said quietly, "When I thought I missed you today . . ."

He didn't finish. Tallie touched his lips and smiled. "When you thought you missed me you used a particular four-letter word. You must have been pretty upset."

Of course Tallie was just teasing Archie, but he pressed his lips together, and closed his eyes as if being hit with guilt. When opening his eyes again he said, "I'm sorry you heard that."

Tallie smiled and said with a little sarcasm, "Well, it was a tense moment."

"Oh, but that wasn't my only slip. I've been yelling curse words at the top of my lungs in my sleep. I guess it's where I've been venting my frustrations. Although that's no excuse. Dream or no dream, it must be somewhere inside of me."

Tallie covered her mouth with her fist, trying to keep a straight face because of how serious Archie was being. She knew his remorse was sincere, and she tried not to find humor in it all, but she finally surrendered to her lighter side and laughed.

"What's so funny?" he asked innocently.

Tallie couldn't answer.

Of course, at this point, Archie was beginning to see the humor in the conversation, and he did enjoy watching Tallie laugh, so he laughed with her until they were finally all laughed out.

Archie smoothed Tallie's hair and said, "You know, I was paid a decent advance for my books, and I was thinking I'd get a place of my own."

"Really?" she asked, wiping the tears of laughter from her face.

Archie continued. "The only thing is I don't think living alone will suit me very well."

Tallie didn't realize his meaning. "I'm sure you'll get used to it, and your parents are right here in town. You'll be fine."

Archie moved closer to Tallie. "I'm not much of a romantic, as I'm sure you've realized by now, but I *was* making fairly romantic preparations for an important question I planned to ask when a certain someone returned from New Zealand."

Tallie was beginning to understand his meaning.

"However, with your unexpected return . . ." Archie stopped and questioned, "You are back to stay?"

Tallie bit her lip and said, "Well, I hadn't planned to. I told Gemma I'd be back after Christmas."

Archie shook his head, "No."

Tallie was surprised at his resolve. "You don't want me to go?"

Archie shook his head again and repeated, "No. Absolutely not." He kissed her forehead. "I don't think living alone will suit me very well, but I do think you might make a good roommate."

"I can't just live with you, Archibald. It goes against my beliefs. You know that."

"No, that came out wrong. I'm not asking you to *just* live with me, Tallie." He laughed. "It goes against my beliefs, too."

"I know," she said.

"Tallulah Z., I was hoping you might agree to marry me."

Tallie's chest began to rise and fall, and she put her hands over her face.

Archie asked, "Is that a good sign . . . or a bad one?"

Tallie took her hands off of her face and wrapped her arms around Archie's ribs, pressing the side of her face against his chest. Archie held Tallie with his free arm and let his cheek rest on the top of her head. They didn't speak but only stood together under Archie's umbrella coming to terms with the confirmation of their love.

While still in an embrace, Archie said, "I'm sorry. I would have had a ring if things would have gone according to . . ."

Tallie unwrapped her arms and put her finger on Archie's lips. "Shhh. I'm the one who messed up your plan. Don't apologize. It's entirely my fault . . . and marrying you would make me the happiest person alive." Shaking her head slowly, she continued. "I've been so lonely since my mom died, and you've made me so happy. I never would have gone to New Zealand if I had seen this in our near future. When I left, you didn't have the book deal, and I didn't see any way I could come live here in Outlandish. Archibald, I left out of desperation. I needed that security. And I kept remembering the promise I made to my mom . . . about not being alone. I wouldn't have left you otherwise. I want you to know that."

"Did Gemma take care of you? Did she make you feel safe and cared for?"

Tallie nodded. "Archibald, I know you don't really like Gemma, and I do get why. I know she has selfish motives sometimes and is definitely too bossy and direct, but she did give me a sense of security I couldn't find anywhere else, and I think God used her to help me when I didn't know what to do with myself."

"I did question her motives," Archie said, "especially when she asked you to go away with her for an entire year, but I'm grateful to her for providing what I couldn't. I did want to, you know. I just didn't know how. My life was just as unstable as yours was."

"I know, Archibald. You were right, though."

"I was right? About what?" he asked.

"You were right about Gemma being unhappy. The night before we both flew away for the holidays, she broke down and cried. Can you believe it?"

Archie's expression revealed compassion. "No, I can't, but I knew there was more to her."

"Yeah, you did. You saw it before I did. She admitted that she'd gotten on the wrong path and wasn't happy with her career or her life. She told me she was going to move on and find out what makes her happy."

"That took a lot of courage," Archie said. "I hope she finds happiness."

"You know what she told me?" Tallie said smiling. "What?"

"She told me you were her first inspiration to leave her career."

"Me?" asked Archie. "How?"

"Yes, *you*," she answered. "She said your perseverance in following your own path, especially in such tough circumstances was enough to make her really look at her own life and look for opportunities that suited her better."

"I can't believe it."

"I can," said Tallie. "You were an inspiration to me from the very first day I met you."

Archie rolled his eyes. "Oh yes, that day on the beach . . . when I ran away from you. I can see how that's very inspiring."

They both laughed and Archie said, "I guess I should thank you for persisting in meeting me. We both know I deserve no credit for that. God knew I'd never meet anyone unless they chased me down."

"It is funny thinking back on it," Tallie admitted.

Archie brushed Tallie's hair away from her face with the back of his hand. "I should also thank you for insisting I write my book, and even calling an agent on my behalf. You know, I never would have been able to ask you to marry me if my career was at a standstill."

"Well, Gemma deserves at least some of the credit for that," Tallie added. "She's the one who gave me Sybil's name and number."

"Yes, I've thought of that," said Archie with a nod.

"And we can't forget Sybil," Tallie added. "After all, she's the one who made your dreams come true. I mean, you are a published author now."

Archie looked tenderly at Tallie. "No Tallie. It was you who made my dreams come true."

Tallie closed her eyes. "This feels like a dream. This is the last thing I expected to happen today."

"You were leaving," Archie added seriously.

Tallie opened her eyes and said seriously, "What about Sybil? Archibald, do you think she has feelings for you, because it sure looked that way to me."

Archie shook his head. "No, she doesn't have feelings for me, but Luke might have found his perfect match."

"Luke?"

Archie nodded. "I don't ever remember seeing him so love-struck, even with Lily."

"Really?" Tallie said with a childish excitement. "That's wonderful! He seemed so sad when I talked to him last. It broke my heart, it really did."

"Yes, well, his being love-struck almost kept me from finding you in time. He came to tell me he saw you yesterday when I was at my book signing, but when he began talking to Sybil he completely forgot why he was there."

Tallie bit her lip. "I ran away from him yesterday. I didn't think he would recognize me with my hat, but then he said my name, and I panicked and took off."

"You thought your hat would disguise you?" Archie asked with a chuckle.

She put the hat on. "Well, what do you think? Would you have recognized me?"

"In a second," he said, cupping her face in his hand.

Tallie looked at Archie with admiration. "I wish I could have been there with you at your signing. I'm so proud of you."

"You could have been there, you know."

"I know. I feel so stupid now. I read everything wrong and messed everything up, didn't I?"

Archie smiled tenderly and shook his head. "No, you didn't.

"Tallie, I prayed God would give you to me, and when you went away I thought he was telling me it wasn't meant to be. I'll admit, I was angry, even at you. I'm sorry for that. I can see now that God was working out a plan that needed to play out just as it did."

Tallie cried again. "I prayed that, too. That God would give you to me. When I called Sybil before I left with Gemma, I really hoped it would lead to a book contract for you. I don't think I could have gone to New Zealand if I hadn't done *something* to give us some hope."

"It worked," Archie said with a nod. "God used that connection to make it possible for us to be together. He answered our prayers, Tallie. He did give us to each other—just as we asked."

Tallie smiled and wiped a few lingering tears with her fingertips. Archie put his arms around her and, leaning down, whispered in her ear, "Tell me again that you love me."

She stood on her toes and whispered in his ear, "I love you, Archibald."

Again he whispered in her ear, "Tell me again that you'll marry me."

Tallie pushed away from his chest and looked up at Archie. "Yes, Archibald Plumby. I will marry you."

Archie smiled warmly and pulled Tallie close once again. She pressed her cheek against his chest, and they stood embracing each other in silence underneath Archie's umbrella. When a few moments passed, Archie stepped back and said to Tallie, "Shall we go and tell Mother and Father?"

Tallie put her hand against her chest. "Mother and Father. I like the sound of that. You know, I only asked God to give me . . . you. But he's also giving me another mother . . . and the father I never had. I don't think I'm coming off this cloud anytime soon."

Archie kissed Tallie on the cheek. Taking her hand from her chest, he placed it on his arm and moved to her side. He leaned down to smile at her and asked, "Shall we?"

PHOTO BY TALLIE GREENLEAF

TEN REASONS
THE *BEACH*
SHOULD BE YOU
NEXT GETAWAY

ACKNOWLEDGMENT
For the story idea and direction, the illustrative vision, and the musical expression, we'd like to give credit to God—the Creator of all Inspiration.

AUTHOR: *Lynnette Kraft* loves a good story, in any form—real or imaginary. She admits to being a dreamer but insists she keeps a level head at the same time. Rather than conniving a way to live in a large beach house in SoCal with a wall of windows facing the beach where she can hear the soothing sounds of the crashing waves . . . she writes about it. It's her escape and her third love. Her first two loves? Her family, the ones she lives for and would die for; and her God, whom she acknowledges as the Giver of Life, Love, Hope and all Inspiration.

ILLUSTRATOR: *Abigail Kraft* is forever nine years old, believes in magic, and likes to draw pictures. She has decided, a childish spirit is her favorite avenue to creativity, so she fills her days with music, family, giggles, daydreams, and animated movies. Then (in true, childish fashion) she cries, grumbles, and sighs her way through unpleasant work, and shows her mom as soon as she's made something she's proud of. Most of all, she loves her Creator, who gave her a super fun life and promises her eternity in the most funnest place of all.

COMPOSER: *Jared Kraft* is a composer for film and media. His passion for music began with experience through listening, moved to expression through piano and eventually arrived at creation through composition. He finds his purpose and inspiration in his perfect Savior, his loving wife, and his wonderful family, and will always value the timeless phenomenon in which organized noise is translated into a universal language.

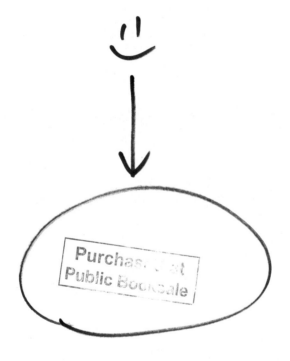

Purchased at
Public Booksale

CPSIA information can be obtained
at www.ICGtesting.com
Printed in the USA
LVOW02s1450010617
536598LV00007B/60/P

9 780991 110926

"You know, you're right! Come to think of it, there was a point where she started letting me get away with it, but I honestly can't tell you when, and I didn't even realize I was calling her by her first name. I guess I've been too stressed out to notice."

"She does like to call the shots, doesn't she?" Archie said sympathetically.

"Yes! She does."

"But you're okay?" Archie asked.

"Yeah, I'm fine."

"That's good," Archie said through a sigh.

They were both quiet for a moment, then Tallie bit her lip and dropped her shoulders. "Um, speaking of Gemma," she said with hesitation. "I want to apologize for the photograph she sold . . . the one of us."

"You don't need to apologize," he said. "It wasn't you who sold the photograph."

"It might as well have been," she answered.

"What do you mean?"

Tallie bit her lip again and thought about changing the subject, but then she felt her face and neck grow warm and knew her bright red splotches would be a dead giveaway to her secret.

"I'm so sorry, Archibald. Gemma did ask me if she could sell it."

Squinting her eyes and turning her face away as if expecting to be rebuked, Tallie added, "She even asked me . . . to ask you."

Archie didn't yet understand the full meaning of her words, but he could tell Tallie had more to say so he waited quietly.

Tallie look down at the table. "See, I knew what your answer would be. I knew it would upset you that she took the picture in the first place, so . . . I didn't ask you, and later I told her *we* didn't mind."

Archie was still confused. "Did I do something to offend you, Tallie?"

"No, no, no. I don't mean I *wanted* to upset you. What I wanted was for you to see the photograph in the paper.

"I've seen your dad reading the *Pacific Coast Buzz*, so I knew there was a good chance you *would* see it."

"I guess I'm missing something. I don't understand," Archie said, narrowing his eyes.

Tallie sighed. "See, I liked the photograph and I thought if you saw us together, you would remember our time together. I wasn't sure I'd see you again so soon, and I . . . well anyway, I am sorry. I know it doesn't make any sense."